The Last Casterglass

D0757236

The Last Casterglass

A Keeping Up with the Penryns Romance

KATE HEWITT

TULE
PUBLISHING

The Last Casterglass
Copyright© 2022 Kate Hewitt
Tule Publishing First Printing, August 2022

The Tule Publishing, Inc.

ALL RIGHTS RESERVED

First Publication by Tule Publishing 2022

Cover design by Rhian

No part of this book may be used or reproduced in any manner
whatsoever without written permission except in the case of brief
quotations embodied in critical articles and reviews.

This is a work of fiction. Names, characters, places, and incidents are
products of the author's imagination or are used fictitiously. Any
resemblance to actual events, locales, organizations, or persons, living or
dead, is entirely coincidental.

ISBN: 978-1-958686-29-4

Dedication

Dedicated to Sophie and Rachel,
my good friends from St Bees!

Chapter One

"DON'T YOU WANT to at least say hello?"

"No." Seph kept her eyes on the gleaming steel spindle of her lathe as her older sister Althea stood in the doorway of her workshop, her hands on her hips, her manner decidedly put out.

"Seph. Come on. This is our first ever intern, and he's going to arrive any minute. We want to make a good impression. Show him we're a united front, a welcoming community—"

A *community*? "Save it, Althea, for the publicity," Seph replied curtly. "I'm working, and it's really difficult to stop a piece in the middle of the process. Anyway, he'll have loads of people to meet right now. I'll say hello later." Maybe.

Althea was silent for a taut moment in which Seph knew she was considering whether to deliver one of her bracing lectures about pulling together for the sake of Casterglass, how everyone needed to do their bit, yada, yada. Seph had already heard versions of this familial Ted Talk at least a dozen times since her older sister had marched back home to take over the family's dilapidated castle nearly a year ago, and tried to turn it into a cross between Legoland and Chatsworth. Somewhat amazingly, she had managed to pull it off, more or less, with everybody else's help. But there were limits to Seph's patience, as well as her willingness to *pull together* with the family who had forgotten she existed for over a decade. And meeting some toffee-nosed fop fresh from Oxford was way down on her list of priorities.

"I'm busy," she stated firmly, just in case her bossy older sister thought she could change her mind with a few well-worn phrases. After another tense moment, Althea gave a huff that was a cross between exasperation and defeat, and then turned and left her workshop without another word.

Seph breathed a sigh of relief, enjoying the spicy smell of cedar that struck her nostrils as she positioned the wood on the main spindle and then adjusted her safety glasses. She was working on a series of outdoor pieces for the Casterglass brand, and hard-wearing cedar was perfect for the flower boxes she was constructing. She ran her hand along the grain of the wood, enjoying the slight roughness of it against her callused palm, knowing she would get it to a satiny finish before she was done. As long as people didn't keep *interrupting* her.

She was about to start up the lathe again when a burst of laughter made her still. She felt the familiar swirl of resentment and longing as she heard the ensuing chatter of voices. The oh so wonderful Oliver Belhaven must have arrived then, she thought with a roll of her eyes, and of course Althea would be rolling out the red carpet. Her older sister was thrilled that Casterglass had attracted the notice of someone asking to be an unpaid intern, and an Oxbridge graduate no less.

Whoop-dee-do, Seph thought, knowing she was being unreasonably bitter, in the privacy of her own mind if not in public. Three years at Oxford and an MA out of it for Master Belhaven, while a year of local sixth form college and zero A levels had been her lot. That wasn't sour grapes, she told herself, not exactly. Who needed a degree, anyway? She was doing just fine.

Conversation continued to float in from the courtyard and Seph started up her lathe again, so the soothing hum of the machinery drowned out any other noise. She *was* busy. This flower box needed finishing. Yet in the pause of the machinery, she heard someone laugh—Althea's fiancé John, she thought, recognising his low, easy rumble—and she felt a little spurt of something—jealousy, perhaps, which was ridiculous, because she'd chosen to stay out here. She knew that, and yet…

It hadn't really felt like a choice. It never did.

She wiped the back of her arm across her forehead and switched off the lathe. The sudden silence that the workshop was plunged into felt absolute; they all must have moved inside, and she couldn't hear a single thing, which should have been a relief but wasn't. Not exactly, anyway. She knew she should stay out here and finish the flower box, if just to prove to Althea she'd meant what she'd said.

And yet, for a reason she couldn't quite fathom and did not want to probe too deeply, Seph found herself moving out into the courtyard, straining her ears. Dusk was falling, violet shadows gathering in the corners, the mountains in the distance no more than jagged black shapes against the darkening horizon.

Ellie, who ran the pottery shop, had left hours ago; now that it was November, she only opened for a few hours on Saturdays and Sundays. They'd had very few visitors since September, after a banner August, when paying customers had flooded through the gates. Althea had big plans for some winter-themed parties and events in November and December, and a big Christmas wedding reception to boot, a prospect that made Seph feel exhausted before she'd even thought about it properly, although she recognised that keeping Casterglass open and offering events was probably the only way to keep the place afloat. And keeping the place afloat had become, since Althea's return, something of a given. Her sister had assumed that was what everyone wanted, because this was Casterglass, after all. The family pile. The ancestral castle. The only home Seph had ever known.

She took a few steps towards that home, taking in the lights in the kitchen, the silhouettes of people moving around. She could picture Olivia filling the big brown teapot, this Oliver Belhaven chatting with John and Will, Olivia's fiancé. Her brother Sam and his girlfriend, no doubt soon-to-be-wife, Rose were at the hospital in Kendal, with their premature twins who had been born a few weeks ago, to much excitement and celebration. Her mother would be wafting around as usual, Seph thought, and her father smiling benignly. Something clenched in her stomach, and she made herself breathe in and out a few times.

Never mind. She didn't want to be there. She turned around to head back to her workshop, only to be stopped by a friendly voice.

"Hey, Seph, aren't you joining us?"

It was John's eighteen-year-old daughter Alice. She and Althea's daughter Poppy were best friends, although Poppy had started university at Lancaster this September while Alice had decided to take a gap year and help out at her father's farm.

"I've got work to do," Seph replied after a second's pause.

Alice raised her eyebrows in scepticism, which made Seph smile, at least a little. She and Alice had known each other for a long time. Seph had started hanging around Appleby Farm when she was about twelve or so, sullen and lonely, and John had taken her under his easy, amicable wing. He'd been the one to teach her woodworking, and although Alice was five years younger than her, they'd always got along.

"Come on, Seph," she said, smiling, "don't be grumpy."

"I'm not grumpy!" Seph replied, indignant. She knew she could come across as abrupt and yes, maybe a bit sullen, but she wasn't *grumpy*.

"Whatever you're doing, I'm sure it can wait. Oliver's really nice. And," she added, her tone turning mischievous, "he's cute. Fit, I mean, but in a slightly geeky way." She grinned. "Just your type."

"Don't," Seph retorted, annoyed to realise she was actually blushing. She turned away to hide the colour that had stupidly flooded into her face. "Some Oxford toff?" she scoffed. "Not my type at all, trust me."

"Oh, I don't know—"

"I do." She strode back towards her workshop. "I'll put my tools away and then come and say hello," she promised, only to placate Alice, and not because she was curious. Not at all.

"All right, but don't be long," Alice replied severely, and then, with a toss of her long, blonde hair, she went back into the kitchen while Seph headed to the safety of her workshop. As she packed away her tools and tidied the shop, she took her time because she was realising she didn't want to burst into the kitchen and have everyone turn to stare at her. That kind of attention was more or less her worst nightmare, which was why she tended to avoid these types of gatherings, or really, *any* types of gatherings. After a childhood spent in virtually complete solitude, coping with a crowd was not yet in her skill set.

But, she acknowledged, as she finished tidying the workshop, she should at least make an appearance. A very quick one, just so she wouldn't be considered *rude*. Or grumpy. With a sigh, Seph glanced around her workshop, taking comfort in the machinery now shrouded in sheets, the warm, spicy smell of wood that still lingered in the air.

Although she had a tangle of complicated feelings about turning Casterglass into a tourist attraction, she did love this workshop. She loved making things with her hands and sharing them with the world—although the sharing part was still a little bit scary. But still, the opportunity to do what she loved was soul-satisfying, a pleasure that resounded in her very bones.

With another sigh she turned off the lights and headed to the house.

❄

WHOA, THERE WERE a *lot* of people here. Oliver kept smiling and nodding as he was introduced to far too many names to remember. Althea he knew, because he'd corresponded with her. Walter and Violet Penryn he recognised from the website, as the twelfth baron of Casterglass and his wife. John was Althea's fiancé. After that the names and faces started to blur. Alice, Will, Toby, John... He just kept smiling.

"So what made you decide to come to Casterglass?" Violet asked, eyebrows raised. She had a decidedly ditzy way about her, but Oliver thought he saw a certain shrewdness in her pale blue eyes.

"I saw a spread in *Country Life* and my curiosity was piqued," he said with yet another smile and an easy-going shrug. "How you turned the place around." He'd been particularly encouraged by how dilapidated Casterglass had looked in the 'before' photos—and still did, in some regards—and how Althea had talked about doing it up on a 'shoestring.' Both aspects appealed to him, and applied to his own faint hopes.

"You've just graduated from Oxford, haven't you?" Walter chimed in with a beaming smile. "Which college?"

"Um, Harris Manchester." He gave an apologetic smile, because it was the college most people hadn't heard of, the one for 'mature' students—that was, anyone over twenty-one. Oliver had been twenty-two when he'd started.

Sure enough, Walter's forehead wrinkled in confusion before he said, almost sadly, "Oh, I was at Brasenose. Wonderful place. Wonderful times."

"Yes, I'm sure. Lovely city—"

The kettle started whistling shrilly and Althea's sister—Olivia?—whisked it off the enormous Aga. Although Casterglass was at least five times the size of Pembury Farm, its kitchen had the same cosy shabbiness that Oliver loved about the home he was desperate to save. Coming to Casterglass was a last-ditch attempt to keep it in the family...and one he already suspected wouldn't work.

"So you mentioned you were the nephew of an earl…?" Althea asked as Olivia poured the tea and they all sat down at the rectangular oak table that looked as if it could seat at least twenty.

"Oh, er, sort of." Oliver felt himself blushing. He'd mentioned the tenuous aristocracy connection out of desperation, but now he felt embarrassed that he'd actually dared to play that worn-out card. "My great-great-uncle was an earl, but the earldom went extinct in the nineteenth century, when there were no male heirs to pass it on to." He gave an apologetic grimace.

"Oh, that's too bad." Althea looked a bit too crestfallen, Oliver thought. Did it make that much difference to her, whether he was related to nobility or not? He was an unpaid intern, after all. "And what is the name of the earldom's seat?"

The earldom's *seat*? He found himself blushing harder and he was grateful for a pause in which to gather his wits while Olivia passed around mugs of tea. He took his own with a murmured thanks, taking a sip before he made himself reply, "The earldom's seat is Pembury Hall, but I'm afraid it was sold after the First World War. It's a hotel now, with a golf course. My uncle owns Pembury Farm, which was the farm attached to the original estate. That's the property I'm looking to…" he paused uncertainly before finishing: "…save."

"I see," Althea said, and Oliver feared she now sounded distinctly cool. Had he misrepresented himself? He was sure he hadn't indicated that his family home was Pembury Hall. He'd never even been in the place; his uncle refused to go, even though it was just down the road.

An awful beat of silence followed before Althea's fiancé—John?—chipped in. "A farm, eh? I'm a farming man myself. Sheep, mainly. What does your uncle farm?"

"Er, nothing, really." This was starting to feel slightly excruciating. Oliver took another sip of tea before continuing. "After the hall and most of the land was sold off, my uncle moved to the farmhouse mainly to save money. He doesn't actually farm, but that's something I'd certainly consider, if I'm able to manage the property."

Another few seconds of silence. Oliver was almost starting to wish he hadn't come. He really hadn't thought he'd misrepresented himself when he'd written to Althea a few months ago, but now he wondered if he had, either subconsciously or unintentionally. Had he made it sound like he was saving Pembury Hall, and not the far more modest farmhouse? And did it really make a difference?

"Well, it all sounds terribly interesting," Violet remarked brightly. "And we certainly look forward to your help for the next few months."

"Thank you. I look forward to helping." Oliver smiled weakly and took yet another sip of tea. Althea, he saw, was frowning slightly, like she couldn't make him out. He supposed it did seem a bit strange, that he'd asked for this internship when the house he wanted to work on was nothing like Casterglass. A six-bedroom farmhouse with outbuildings and about ten acres was a far cry from the likes of this castle, but it was Oliver's home, his heart. And if he logged these hours and gained some of the experience his uncle claimed he didn't have, then maybe he wouldn't sell Pembury Farm like he was threatening to.

"Well, I'm sure you'll be very useful," Althea said a bit dubiously. Oliver was saved from having to reply by the kitchen door swinging open hard and banging against the wall. A young woman stood there, scowling and looking fierce. Oliver stared at her in surprise, for she was unlike any of the other Penryns he'd met so far. Her hair was possibly the most extraordinary thing about her—bright pink dreadlocks that were growing out so there was about four inches of platinum-blonde hair at her roots. Her face was heart shaped with bright blue-green eyes and an expression of deep discontent. Her body, slender and willowy, was swathed in a pair of baggy, paint-splattered dungarees, paired with well-worn work boots.

"Seph," Olivia exclaimed, sounding genuinely delighted. "Come meet Oliver."

The woman's gaze swung towards him, looking decidedly unfriendly. "Hello." She sounded sulky, and as he often did, Oliver found himself overcompensating. He sprang up from the table, nearly spilling his tea.

"So pleased to meet you!" He came out from around the table, holding out his hand to shake, while she looked at it like it was something dead, and everyone looked on in bemusement. "I'm Oliver. And you're...Seth?"

"Seph," she replied, with a touch of scorn.

"Short for Persephone," Olivia filled in helpfully. "Mum is a classicist."

"It was such a disappointment that your father wouldn't let me call Sam Amphitryon," Violet said, a touch mournfully. "He was such a moving figure. He rescued Thebes from the Teumessian fox, you know."

"There are limits," Walter replied genially. "And there have been Samuels in the Penryn line for over three hundred years. It's my middle name," he explained to Oliver, who could only nod. Seph still hadn't taken his hand, and he had no choice but to rather sheepishly withdraw it.

"Anyway, nice to meet you," he said again, and then, because he didn't know what else to do, he slunk back to his seat.

She didn't bother to reply.

"Seph, come and have some tea," Olivia entreated, and Oliver had the sense she was talking to some wild creature in need of taming. After a second's pause Seph moved over to the enormous brown teapot and poured herself a mug. Oliver watched as she poured milk in and no less than three sugars. She leaned against the counter and sipped it, gazing around watchfully at them all over the rim of her mug.

The conversation moved back, unfortunately, to him and his circumstances.

"So what exactly are you hoping to do with Pembury Farm?" Althea asked and Oliver had the urge to squirm, which he thankfully resisted.

"Uh, well, keep it in the family, basically," he said. "Some of the ideas you've implemented here could work on the farm, I think. The campsite, in particular, and the workshops. I've also thought about having pick-your-own vegetables and fruit—there are orchards on the property—apple, plum, and cherry."

Althea's expression had turned thoughtful as she sipped her tea. "Pick your own. I like that."

"We've let the orchard go a bit, I'm afraid," Walter told him with an apologetic smile. "I don't think the trees are very productive anymore."

"I don't even know where the orchard is," Olivia exclaimed. "Where is it, Daddy?"

"Across the river, on the far side of the wood, opposite the campsite."

"Perhaps that's something Oliver can help with," a young woman—John's daughter?—suggested. "Getting the orchard back into shape."

"You can't prune trees in autumn, I'm afraid," John put in, with a commiserating look for Oliver, as if he would have known that. The truth was, he'd thrown the 'pick-your-own' idea out there a bit wildly, simply because Pembury Farm did have a somewhat productive orchard. He didn't know the first thing about fruit trees, however. So great, yet another way he could feel like a fake.

"In January though," Althea said musingly. "You'll still be here then, won't you, Oliver?"

The terms of his internship—unpaid as it was—had been decidedly ambiguous. "Possibly," he said, trying to sound optimistic. Would Uncle Simon have decided on whether to sell by then? He kept making ominous noises, but Oliver didn't know if that was just his way to keep him guessing. As long as he didn't sell, he knew Oliver was beholden to him, willing to dance to his tune. But once he did…

Well, it simply didn't bear thinking about.

Oliver straightened and smiled around at the group, determined to stay optimistic. Uncle Simon had said he needed experience to run Pembury Farm, and so here he was, gaining it. He'd work hard and learn along the way, and never mind the slight missteps he'd had so far. Too much was riding on this to let himself be dissuaded by a little disapproval.

As if sensing his thoughts, Seph caught his eye and gave him a scowl. Oliver's benign smile faltered. For a second, she looked as if she actively hated him, and the optimism he'd been holding on to so determinedly slipped, just a little. Three months suddenly seemed like a rather long time.

Chapter Two

OLIVER WOKE TO a torrential downpour hammering the roof of his attic bedroom. Olivia had shown him to his room last night, slightly apologetic about the fact that he was being housed in the former servants' quarters.

"All the rooms in the addition are taken at the moment," she explained, "since everyone is living at home. But once Althea moves to Appleby Farm after the wedding, you might be able to have her bedroom."

Take the intimidating Althea's bedroom? No thanks. Oliver had assured her he was fine in the servants' quarters; there was no one else up under the eaves, and the bathroom down the hall, with its Victorian tub and trickle of rust-coloured water, was his alone.

Now, in the morning, Oliver stared at the ceiling as a gloomy, grey light filtered through the curtains. He tried to recapture some of the ebbing optimism he'd felt last night. He was a bit overwhelmed by all the Penryns with their various eccentricities; he'd grown up with his one cousin Jack who had gone to boarding school at seven, when Oliver had been only five years old. Life at Pembury Farm with his uncle had been decidedly quiet, save for the dreaded intervals when his cousin came home. In between those times, however, his uncle had been a man of few words and his aunt Penny, who was a far more convivial character, had divorced Simon and moved to London when Oliver had been twelve. He still kept in touch with her, and she was as fun and enthusiastic as ever, if a bit distant.

The women in his life, he'd thought more than once, with a determined pragmatism, seemed destined to leave him—first his own mother, scarpering off to Australia when he was a kid, and then his aunt and virtual mother figure. And then there was Audrey, who had decided, regretfully it was true, that they had no future after two years together at Oxford. Hopefully it wouldn't become a continuing trend, but the truth was he hadn't had much luck in the romance department so far. For some reason this made him think of the mysterious Seph, with her blue-green eyes and ferocious scowl. No joy there certainly, he thought with a sigh, and yet he still wondered. Why had she seemed so angry?

Shaking himself free of such pointless, meandering thoughts, he rose from the bed to brave the icy, bare floorboards and then the barely lukewarm trickle of the shower. Five-star accommodation it was not, but he wasn't going to complain. Free room and board had been generous enough for him.

Twenty minutes later, wearing a button-down shirt and

brown cords, his hair still damp, he ventured down to the kitchen in search of breakfast and his boss—last night Althea had mentioned eight a.m. as a potential start time. It was twenty to now.

The kitchen was, somewhat surprisingly, empty, although people had clearly eaten, judging by the tottering pile of dirty dishes in the sink. Hesitating for a moment, unsure how at home he should make himself, Oliver finally went in search of toast and tea, thankfully finding both without too much difficulty. He'd just sat down to his breakfast when Althea blew into the kitchen on a wind of purposeful determination.

"Ah, Oliver! There you are. Making yourself at home?"

"Sorry—" Oliver began, his mouth full of toast, but Althea brushed aside his uncertain apology.

"No, no, I'm glad." She glanced at her watch. "When you've finished eating, I thought you could have a wander around the property, poke your nose in where you like. Just to get the feel of the place. Then we can sit down and talk about what you'll actually do. We've never had an intern before, so all ideas and suggestions gratefully accepted." She let out a laugh, which made Oliver wonder if she'd been joking. She seemed like the sort of person to have a minute-by-minute timetable, which she would stick to down to the second.

"Great," he said, since she seemed to be waiting for a response, and with a brisk nod she turned on her heel and walked out.

Oliver turned back to his toast. He munched in silence for a few minutes before the door banged open, just as it had last night, and Seph stood there, with the same scowl. Good grief, was her face frozen in that grimace? He was reminded of his aunt Penny telling him not to make funny faces, in case one of them stuck. Seph's seemed to have done just that.

"Good morning," he said, swallowing the last of his toast, and she just glared at him before striding, loose and long-limbed, to the kettle. Today she was wearing a pair of heavy work trousers, the kind you might wear while chain-sawing, and a voluminous plaid shirt, its sleeves rolled up to the elbows to reveal slender arms, skinny wrists. As she reached for the kettle, Oliver thought there was something strangely, endearingly vulnerable about the sight of those wrists—so pale and slender, so incongruous with the tough-ness of the rest of her.

"I just filled it," he told her, keeping his tone bright. "It should still be hot."

In reply Seph switched the kettle on, with a loud click. Oliver blinked. Stupid to feel like turning on a kettle was something of a rebuff, and yet…was it?

"What do you do around Casterglass?" he asked, reaching for his tea. "From what I learned last night, everyone seems to have their own area of responsibility."

She turned around to face him, leaning against the counter and folding her arms as the kettle, having boiled, clicked off almost instantly, which gave Oliver a small, perverse, and rather childish sort of pleasure.

"I run the woodworking shop," she stated, and then turned around again to make her tea. Oliver watched her, wondering if she was like this with everyone, or if it was just him.

"I look forward to seeing it," he said, wishing he didn't sound quite so...enthusiastic. It was a habit he had learned in childhood, to overcompensate for his uncle's silences. He turned just the tiniest bit manic, hyper-friendly, ridiculous. It had not been a good look in primary school, and it wasn't now, either.

Seph was giving him a rather disbelieving look, which made him explain, a bit stiffly, "Althea mentioned that I'd be spending time with each area of the estate's interests. So I suppose I'll make it to woodworking at some point."

She snorted—actually snorted—and then dumped her teabag into the sink before striding back outside without a word. Good *grief.* Oliver's irritation at such behaviour warred with a needling hurt he told himself to dismiss. Persephone Penryn clearly had the attitude problem, not him. He'd try to steer clear of her as much as he could, and get to know some of the other dozen or so people who seemed to be living on site.

And he'd start by doing what Althea had said, and exploring the estate—making sure to avoid the woodworking shop, of course.

✳

SEPH GRITTED HER teeth, fighting a flush of mortification as she strode as quickly as she could from the kitchen, back to the safety of her shop. She'd handled *that* badly. Really badly, if the shocked expression on Oliver's face was anything to go by. He probably thought she was unbelievably rude, not to mention pathetically lacking in social skills. Both, she thought dispiritedly, were true, although it wasn't just a lack of social skills that had made her be so abrupt with Oliver Belhaven; it had been fear. It was always fear, not that she'd ever admit it to anyone.

She was afraid of actually trying with someone and being rebuffed. Rejected. She'd had enough of that to last a lifetime, and so over the years it had become easier not to try, with anyone. A few people had managed to breach her defences—John Braithwaite being one, when he'd let her help out with the farm as a moody teenager. But with most people Seph knew, her default was to act like she didn't care, because the more she acted like she didn't, the easier she could convince herself it was true. And now it basically was...sort of, except too often things still hurt, even if she tried not to let them.

Anyway, Oliver Belhaven was a random stranger who would be gone in three months, so she really *didn't* care what he thought. Right? Except last night he'd seemed so—well, like Alice had said, *cute*. In an endearing way, weirdly lovably eager to please, and yet also...undeniably fit. There was that,

Seph couldn't deny.

When it came to romance, her experience with the opposite sex was next to nil, and yet she'd still noticed. The floppy dark hair. The bright green eyes twinkling behind wire-rimmed glasses. The body, that even in boring button-down shirts and cords had looked lean and well-muscled. Yes, she'd definitely noticed, even if she'd done her best to act as if she hadn't, as if she couldn't care less, which she couldn't, of course, because...*well*. There was absolutely no point thinking about Oliver Belhaven that way. She had made just about the worst impression she could have, and that was probably a mercy. He'd certainly steer clear of her now. A fact that should bring relief—and did—along with a tiny, irritating, needling disappointment.

Seph pushed that feeling away as she shut the door of her shop and reached for her safety goggles, determined to lose herself in her work for a good few hours—and not think of Oliver Belhaven once.

❄

BY ELEVEN O'CLOCK her muscles were aching, her face flecked with sawdust, as she turned off the lathe, took off her safety goggles, and gave a long, languorous stretch. The flower box was finished, and it looked good, if she did say so herself. She put her hands to the small of her back as she peered out the window of her shop at the courtyard that was still swathed in gloom, although the downpour of earlier had downgraded to a mizzling drizzle. Still it was—as it always was in November, as well as about nine other months of the year—cold, wet, and grey.

She wondered what Oliver Belhaven thought of the good old Cumbrian weather, and then was annoyed at herself for immediately going there. She hadn't thought of him once while working, absorbed in the smooth flow of wood underneath her hands, but the minute she'd stopped, her brain inevitably went to that place. Why? Just because he was a good-looking guy? Admittedly she hadn't come across many of those, stuck at Casterglass for her entire life.

Letting out a groan of frustration at her own thoughts, Seph decided to take a break and grab a coffee from the café across the courtyard. Her brother Sam's girlfriend Rose had transformed it into a cosy and welcoming space, with leather sofas and shelves full of books, plus a full menu of cakes and pastries, as well as some truly delicious coffee. Since it was November, the café was closed but Seph had learned to operate the espresso machine—not all that different from a lathe, if you looked at it a certain way. One big piece of machinery was very much like another.

She stepped into the empty café, flicking on the lights before turning to the espresso machine. The sound of the machine was loud in the stillness of the empty café, and as she waited for the coffee to brew, she felt a sudden, familiar sweep of homesickness—a feeling that came over her at unexpected times, in quiet, solitary moments, like being lost in a fog, or carried away on a tide. How could you be homesick when you were already home? Seph wondered, far from the first time, and yet she knew she was.

Homesick not so much for a place, but for a feeling or maybe a situation. For *something*, and she hadn't yet figured out what it was. The Germans had a word for it, she'd learned—*sehnsucht*, defined as a wistful longing for a place or time, an indefinable yearning or desire. More and more Seph found herself experiencing this, like an ache that ran right through her, which left her feeling emptier than before and yet longing to be filled, and she didn't know how to make it go away.

Shaking her head at such foolishly fanciful thoughts, she poured the foamed milk on top of her espresso and added her usual three sugars. She'd get back to work and stop indulging these stupid emotions. She didn't know why she'd turned so fanciful all of a sudden. It was definitely out of character.

She turned off the machine and the lights and then headed back to the comfort and safety of her workshop— only to stop stock-still in the doorway, in complete and horrified disbelief, at the sight of Oliver Belhaven nosing around her things, completely unashamed of his unabashed prying.

He was wandering around her shop, touching her tools, inspecting her pieces, as if he had every right to be there. As she stood there, utterly shocked, she saw with an icy sort of incredulity that he was lifting a dustsheet from a sculpture tucked away in the back corner of the shop—one that was not for sale or public consumption. She watched as he ran his hand down the side of it—*Out of the Wild*, her most private, personal piece; one she could hardly bear to look at herself, because it felt so revealing.

Her whole body was trembling and yet she could not make herself speak. Standing there, without him even seeing her, she felt utterly exposed, as if she were stark naked. Oliver turned then, a look of surprise on his face, as if he hadn't expected her to show up in her own workshop.

"Oh, hello! I was just having a look around. This is quite nice—what do you call it?"

He ran his hand down the length of *Out of the Wild* again, and Seph had the unsettling sensation that he'd just touched her. Intimately. Unasked, unwanted, like an assault.

For another few seconds she couldn't speak. She was holding her coffee cup so tightly that the hot liquid had sloshed out, burning her hand. She felt stripped down, laid bare, her most intimate self unbearably scrutinised…and he didn't even seem to realise it, which was both a relief and even more of an affront. How could he expose her like this and not even *know*?

"Get—out," she finally managed to squeeze out of her constricted throat. Oliver looked startled, then bemused.

"Sorry, should I not have come in? I did knock—"

"Get—out—now." It was all she could manage. She

turned away from him, tears blurring her eyes, her whole body shaking. It was an overreaction. She knew that full well, and Oliver wouldn't understand it at all, but it didn't matter. She couldn't keep herself from it. No one had seen that sculpture. *No one.* She'd carved it out of her own soul, created from the deepest, darkest parts of herself formed into wood, and he was looking at it as if it were some pretty trinket. Next he'd be asking her how much she wanted for it.

"Seph, look, I'm sorry—" He sounded both taken aback and genuinely apologetic, but at this point she didn't care. Couldn't.

"Just get out!" she half-screamed, the words torn from her throat. Tears were starting in her eyes, but her back was to him, so she hoped and prayed he couldn't see. "Please." She managed to lower her voice to something that almost sounded rational. "Please, just…leave."

A few seconds passed, taut and quiet. The only sound was Oliver's breathing—or maybe that was her own, coming in ragged gasps. Her heart was thundering. He was going to think she was an absolute basket case, beyond hope or help, but in this moment Seph knew she just needed to be alone. Immediately.

"I'm sorry," he said again, quietly this time, meaning it, and then he walked out of her shop, closing the door behind him with a click.

Seph let out a trembling sob as she fell to her knees and buried her head in her arms. She didn't know what was worse—that Oliver Belhaven had seen her sculpture, or that she'd freaked out on him over it. Either way it all felt awful, unbearable. She never wanted to lay eyes on him again, and yet he was here for three months, knowing her secrets without even realising that he did, thinking she was crazy. How on earth was she going to cope?

Chapter Three

OLIVER STOOD BY the door to Seph's shop and listened to her breath come in tearing gasps that sounded alarmingly close to sobs. He had *not* been expecting that reaction. He hesitated, then half-turned to go back inside, only to stop with his hand on the door. It had been abundantly clear that she wanted to be alone. He was a stranger, and she did not need him intruding into her moment of—what? Grief? Sorrow? Anger? He didn't even understand why.

Slowly Oliver traced his steps back out of the courtyard. He didn't feel like going back into the castle, now that the rain had mostly cleared, and so he decided to head into the walled garden, which he'd learned was Olivia's domain. In November it was brown and bare, everything neatly tended but dormant, dead-looking. Oliver wandered through the winding paths, his mind on Seph.

Why on earth had she reacted like that?

All right, yes, maybe he shouldn't have walked into her shop uninvited the way he had. Guilt prickled through him uncomfortably at the realisation. The trouble was, he'd been on his own all morning, poking his nose into all the dusty rooms of the castle as the rain had poured down. He'd got used to having a good old nosy—opening drawers, taking books from shelves, riffling through various cabinets and cupboards, all with Althea's blessing. It had been interesting, in an abstract sort of way, although he'd felt very removed from the people of Casterglass with Pembury Farm on his mind.

Someone had helpfully put little plaques in each of the main rooms detailing the history of the castle and its barons—from the first in the fourteenth century, who had been given the castle as a wedding gift, to the dissolute ones during the Tudor period and the rogue one who sent troops to the Parliamentarians besieging Carlisle in the English Civil War. He'd learned about how one baron in the Victorian age had made some important scientific discovery—something about an element—and how the current baron's grandfather had built part of the addition where the family now resided.

All in all it had been interesting but a bit lonely, and completely irrelevant to his own cause because he couldn't turn Pembury's farmhouse into a tourist attraction; it wasn't big enough. It was the land and the barns he needed to develop, and so when the rain had downgraded to a drizzle he'd headed outside with a determined spring in his step.

By that time, though, he'd got used to going where he pleased, and so when he'd seen Seph's woodworking shop empty, the door left temptingly ajar, he hadn't thought twice.

Oliver faltered in his step as an innate honesty compelled him to acknowledge that that wasn't *precisely* true. He *had* paused on the threshold, wondering if he should go in, and yet feeling remarkably curious about the woman with startling eyes and pink dreadlocks. Wanting to know more about her, something she, in her prickliness, wouldn't reveal. And so he'd tiptoed in, and closed the door quietly behind him, and poked around, knowing, at least in part, that she probably wouldn't want him there.

He still hadn't anticipated such an over-the-top reaction, though.

By this time he'd made his way through the bare-walled garden, to a gate on the other side. Decorative wooden signs directed him to the campsite up the hill or to the beach, following a path along the river. He wondered if Seph had made them, and thought she probably had.

Recalling what Walter had said last night about the orchard, he decided to ignore the pretty signs and strike out on his own, up the hill and to the east, where the apple trees were meant to be. As he hiked higher and higher, his thoughts remained on Seph.

How could he make it better? Clearly he needed to apologise. The sculpture he'd peeked at had been extraordinary, but it must have been private. It had been under a dust sheet, after all. Still, Oliver had meant what he'd said—he'd liked it. Moreover, he'd been fascinated by it—the way the rough, unhewn wood transformed seamlessly into a silky, burnished sculpture. A tangle of vines bursting forth, curving upwards, some rough, some smooth, like an explosion in a heart, a sunburst in the mind. There had been something raw and powerful about it, starkly beautiful but also a little—despairing? There had been a kind of yearning to it, perhaps. He didn't know exactly, but staring at that sculpture had made him experience a tangle of powerful emotions, and he wished he'd been able to communicate that to Seph, to explain to her how moving he'd found it. Instead he'd said something remarkably stupid about it being quite nice. How inane could he be? No wonder she'd freaked out on him; except her reaction still took him by surprise.

She hadn't been angry, as he might have expected, but more…heartbroken. And that was his fault.

He'd reached the top of the hill now, breathing hard, the air damp and cold. The heavy grey banks of clouds were starting to clear to reveal pale patches of blue, and a weak, watery sunlight made the river below glint as it wound its way towards the sea. Oliver turned east.

He wasn't entirely sure if he'd find the orchard, or if it would be overgrown by the spruce and larch covering much of the ground, but he was determined now to look for it. He'd apologise to Seph, he decided as he walked, and tell her what he really thought about the sculpture. He doubted she'd take kindly to either sentiment, but it still felt like the right thing to do. And he wouldn't go into her workshop again, not if she didn't invite him. But considering the kind of reactions he'd generated so far, he doubted she would.

The woodland tapered off and Oliver let out a puff of satisfaction as he saw what had to have been the Casterglass orchard, once upon a time. There were apple trees, knobbly and bent over like old women, in desperate need of pruning, brambles growing all the way up to their lower branches. Damson and cherry too, and even pear. He ran his hand along the trunk of a tree, wondering if he could possibly help bring this orchard back to life. Give something back to Casterglass, rather than just take the experience he needed to prove to his uncle he was capable of running Pembury Farm.

It was starting to rain again, a cold, needling sort of spray, and so regretfully, he turned back towards the castle. He supposed he should find Althea and figure out what was next. He was also still thinking about Seph, and how he could approach her.

As he came out of the walled garden, he ran into Althea's fiancé John, carrying some boards towards the barn. His craggy face split into a smile as he caught sight of him.

"Oliver! How are you finding it?"

"I've had a good old ramble," Oliver replied, smiling back. He appreciated John's easy manner, his unassuming friendliness. "I found the orchard."

"Did you? Well done! Is it as bad as I think?"

"Probably. Brambles everywhere, and the trees in desperate need of pruning. Not," he added quickly, "that I'm an expert. Not even close."

"I'm sure you know more than most of the Penryns," John replied with a wink. "They're all pretty lovably clueless, save maybe Seph."

Oliver took a deep breath. No time like the present. "Speaking of Seph, do you know where she is?"

John's eyebrow rose but he made no remark about Oliver's question except to say, "In her workshop, most likely, but I'd give her a little space if I were you. She seemed in a foul mood when I came across her about fifteen minutes ago, even for her." His smile was full of affection as he added, "I know she seems quite forbidding, but she can be quite the softie, really, inside. I don't know what's got her all het up this time."

Oliver grimaced and then decided he needed to come clean. "I'm afraid I have. I went into her workshop without asking and had a poke around while she wasn't there." The look of surprise on John's face made Oliver realise afresh just how presumptuous he'd been. "I wasn't thinking, not exactly. I'd been poking around all morning at Althea's request, and I suppose I just carried on." He didn't feel he could explain to John how he'd also been curious. True confessions only extended so far, especially with near-strangers.

John nodded slowly. "Well, I can understand why Seph wouldn't like that, certainly."

"Yes." Oliver's grimace deepened. He wasn't going to mention peeking at that sculpture, either. "I wanted to apologise—"

"I'd leave it if I were you. Seph is one of those people who needs time on her own. She'll come around, but I'd give it a few hours. Better yet, a few days."

A few days? Oliver couldn't hide his dismay. He'd wanted it sorted, so they could both move on. Maybe even become friends, of a sort, although at this point that seemed unlikely.

"All right," he said reluctantly. "I suppose."

John hesitated, and then laid a hand on Oliver's shoulder. "Seph is a great girl. She's had a pretty difficult time of it—not that anyone even knows. I don't think she'd like me telling you that much, and so I'm not going to say anything more, except...give her the benefit of the doubt, if you can. And be patient with her."

Oliver blinked, both surprised and touched by the older man's advice. "All right," he said, because what else could he say? Yet right now he felt like Seph was the one who needed to be patient with him.

✳

SEPH DIDN'T KNOW how long she knelt on the cold, hard floor of her workshop, trying not to cry, but at some point, her legs started to ache, and she sniffed back the last of her tears as she scrambled up to standing. She'd spilled most of her coffee and the rest was cold, so she hurled it into the trash before covering up *Out of the Wild* again, and then, recklessly, bundling it up and taking it right out of the shop.

John greeted her in passing as she marched across the courtyard, and she snarled something back, too raw to make an effort, even with him. Then she went into the woods skirting the drive, shouldering her way through the massive rhododendrons, to the old icehouse she didn't think anyone knew about, and thrust the sculpture in there. The damp wouldn't be great for it, but she'd find a better place to put it soon. Right now she just needed it out of sight—hers as well as anyone else's. It reminded her too much of what she didn't have, and also what she hoped for. The thought of Oliver seeing it, perhaps guessing something of that, made everything in her cringe and cramp.

Back in her workshop she grabbed her goggles and a hunk of cedarwood and set to work. She was making a domed planter and she intended to put all her energy and focus into it. Work was the only thing that silenced her mind, quieted her heart. It would keep her from thinking about the irritating Oliver Belhaven.

And it did, for a little while, but then just as before, as soon as she'd switched off the lathe and wiped the sawdust and sweat from her forehead, he came back again. Why had he snooped in her private space? And what did he think about her now? How was she going to face him again, ever?

It was lunchtime, and usually Olivia put on soup and

bread for everyone in the kitchen. It tended to be a good time to check in, have a chat, and Seph actually enjoyed it—sort of—not that she ever said so. Today, however, she was dreading it. Oliver was sure to be there, and she was really not ready to see him. She hadn't decided how she was going to play it—ignore him completely, or make her displeasure clear in a pointed sort of way, or just pretend it hadn't happened and simply be normal, whatever *that* looked like.

That was the trouble, Seph thought dispiritedly, of having such limited social experience. She just didn't *know*.

Still, she was starving, so she decided to brave whatever awaited her in the kitchen. By the time she got there, everyone had already sat down with steaming bowls of soup, and there was a loaf of fresh bread—Olivia loved baking—in the middle of the table. Seph's stomach growled, and her heart leapt with relief when she saw that Oliver was not present. Neither was Althea.

"They're having a working lunch in Althea's office," Violet said like it was an answer, although Seph hadn't actually asked anything. "Oliver and Althea," she added helpfully. "In case you were wondering where they were."

"I wasn't," Seph replied shortly, and sat down.

It made her wonder how obvious she was being, if her dotty mother had figured out she was looking for Oliver. What if he'd *said* something? *What on earth is wrong with Seph?* he might have asked, all puzzled innocence. *She practically tore me a new one after I looked in her little work-*

shop. Is she, you know, all right?

The possibility made Seph suppress a deep-seated shudder.

"Everything okay, darling?" Walter asked with one of his gently whimsical smiles, and Seph gave the answer she always did, because as loving as her father could be, he missed so much, and she knew he never even realised it.

"Yeah," she said, and reached for a slice of hot, fresh bread. "Everything's fine."

THE CLOUDS HAD cleared away, leaving pale blue skies like washed denim, and so after lunch Seph decided to leave her workshop for a bit and clear her head with a long, brisk walk. She'd spent a *lot* of time walking the grounds of Casterglass, and she knew every inch like the back of her own hand, her own soul.

Now she avoided the garden and woods—Sam was working up near the campsite, clearing brush—and headed for a part she doubted anyone would venture into, the tangled rhododendron wood past the icehouse where she'd put her sculpture. There was something otherworldly and middle-earthy about the twisted, knobbly branches, the wide, flat leaves that drooped down in winter, for protection.

Seph had walked through the maze of bushes many times, and knew just where to step, duck, or jump. Ten minutes later she was out on the other side, with a sweep of tufty grass stretching to the nearest fell, a heather-and-gorse-covered incline that stretched to the sky.

She walked quickly, arms swinging, heart pumping, breath coming in frosty puffs that felt invigorating. This was what she needed—to clear her head, to get away from Casterglass and all its demands, all it represented. Here she wasn't sullen Seph, the left-behind child, the one everyone said, "Oh, *Seph*," as if her existence had slipped their mind—again. She wasn't weird or prickly or difficult or simply forgotten. Here she was just herself.

She felt capable and strong, climbing that hill, taking long, purposeful strides. On the way back she'd get her sculpture out of the icehouse and put it back in its place. She'd start locking her workshop, if need be, but damned if she'd let Oliver Belhaven or anyone else make her hide more than she already was.

She reached the top of the fell and breathed in deep. Above her the sky, now a deep, bright blue, stretched away endlessly. In the distance the sea glinted, ruffled with white waves, and seagulls circled and squawked overhead. Here she couldn't even see Casterglass Castle; the Scots pines fringing the rhododendrons were taller than its towers. All she could see was wood, sea, and sky, and it made her feel free. Strong. She could go back there and handle Oliver Belhaven and whatever else came her way, without freaking out or getting weirdly emotional. She *would*.

The sky was starting to darken at its edges, like the edges of a parchment curling up, and she realised she must have been walking for hours. She started down the fell, knowing full well how dangerous it was to be up there when dusk came, even for someone as experienced as herself.

When she'd turned eighteen, she'd started volunteering with Mountain Rescue; John did it, as well, and he had encouraged her to join. While she hadn't been called out all that often, she had enjoyed feeling helpful and capable, assisting climbers, usually city dwellers who had underestimated the power of nature, who had become stuck, lost, or both. The camaraderie had been nice too; most of the other volunteers were men, older than herself, and they'd had a matey yet paternal attitude that Seph had been comfortable with. She'd stopped, though, last year, when Althea had come back and Casterglass looked like it would take all her time.

It was another hour before she was at the icehouse, claiming her sculpture, and then heading back to the workshop with it tucked under her arm. She opened the door cautiously, half-expecting Oliver to be snooping yet again, but of course he wasn't. It wasn't until she'd put her sculpture back where it belonged that she realised he had been in her workshop, after all.

On the stool by the door there was a massive fudge brownie wrapped in wax paper and a note, her name on the envelope, in an elegant scrawl.

Feeling both curious and apprehensive, Seph slipped the single piece of paper from the envelope.

Dear Seph, I'm so sorry for violating the privacy of your workshop. I could say I wasn't thinking about what I was doing but that wouldn't really be true. In all honesty, I was curious, and I wanted to know more about you, so I looked. And what I saw, I really, really liked, even if I wasn't meant to see it. Although liked isn't actually the right word—I was moved, because there was something so raw and powerful and really rather wonderful about it. Maybe that's too much information for you right now, but all this to say I really am sorry, and I hope I can make it up to you—and not just with this brownie. Maybe a coffee in town? Oliver

Seph read through the note twice before she slowly lowered it, staring into space. She really hadn't expected *that*—and she had no idea how to respond. Her mind still spinning, she reached for the brownie, unwrapped it from its paper, and took a massive bite.

Oliver Belhaven was full of surprises, it seemed, and really rather alarming—and strangely exciting—ones.

Chapter Four

"SO WE'LL START with the boring stuff, and get it out of the way first."

Althea gave Oliver a bracing, rather beady-eyed smile, which he did his best to return genially, although the truth was, he wasn't entirely feeling it. He'd spent six hours yesterday closeted with Althea in her office while she went through the endless minutiae of running Casterglass, and while it was, for the most part, quite interesting, he hadn't been able to stop thinking about Seph and wondering how to apologise.

When Althea had finally released him, his mind full of paperwork, he'd decided a note was the way to go, along with some small, innocuous token of his regard. Flowers felt too romantic and so he'd settled on a brownie, driving all the way to Broughton-in-Furness—he hadn't realised *quite* how remote Casterglass actually was—to pick one up from a bakery there—the fudgiest, squidgiest one he could find, not that he even knew Seph liked that kind. Maybe she didn't like brownies at all. Maybe she was gluten-free, or allergic to chocolate, or something like that. Considering his luck so far, she probably was. He could picture her already, fuming as she thrust the brownie towards him.

How dare you give me a brownie!

The image almost made him smile, except that it actually seemed possible.

And what about the note? He'd meant to write something brief and easy—*Sorry, Seph!* and leave it at that—but when he'd begun writing a whole bunch of other stuff had come out. He'd tried to temper the blatant outpouring of emotion with a more casual offer of coffee—although maybe it didn't come across as casual; maybe she thought it was a date. A prospect that he realised both pleased and worried him, in just about equal measure, because maybe it sort of was. Or was he crazy? He barely knew this woman. She most likely near-on despised him. He wasn't sure he even *liked* her, full stop.

And yet...

"Oliver? Hello? Are you listening?"

Oliver forced his mind back to Althea and her explanation of why she was going to start him off with the most boring aspect of the business—filing her mountains of paperwork. So everything else he got to do would seem interesting, he supposed, but it would have been nice to have something to whet his appetite just a *little* more. She'd mentioned getting him involved in marketing, maintaining their website, running the café, helping out on the campsite… Any of those would have been better than sitting in this broom cupboard cum office dealing with old bills.

"Yes, sorry, sorry, I'm listening." He gave Althea a bright smile. "Filing. Brilliant. Yes. Always good to get that out of the way first, see where you are. Clean desk, clean mind, and all that."

He stopped abruptly as Althea gave him a rather narrowed look before reaching for a high stack of bills and invoices. "You can start with these."

Seph hadn't said anything about the brownie at dinner, Oliver reflected a bit glumly as he started on the pile of papers. Althea had disappeared to do something more important, which at least left him alone with his thoughts— and a *lot* of papers. Her filing system was very neatly labelled, but it soon became apparent that she didn't actually ever file anything. The hanging folders in the impressive oak cabinets were practically empty, so Oliver had nearly a year of paperwork to painstakingly go through, which was most likely why she'd given him the unenviable task.

It gave him time to think, at least, and recall that at dinner last night Seph had neither studiously avoided him nor made any effort to meet his gaze, offer a smile of acknowledgement, *anything*. She'd basically acted as if he wasn't even on her radar, which he probably wasn't. She in all likelihood hadn't given him a single thought, thrown the brownie in the bin, and the note as well, before turning back to her lathe.

He really needed to stop obsessing about this, Oliver decided. He wasn't even sure he liked Seph as a *person*, never mind anything more significant. She was grumpy and sullen and, frankly, downright rude. He knew he had a tendency to want people to like him, probably harking back to his childhood abandonment issues—he didn't need therapy to realise that much—but couldn't he manage without sulky Seph's regard?

Then he thought of John's advice—*give her the benefit of the doubt, if you can. And be patient with her.*

And that made him wonder. Quite a bit. What sort of difficult time had Seph had? And just how difficult had it been? What, really, made her the way she was—seemingly ready to lash out at anyone and everyone, out of defence, perhaps, or maybe fear? And what was it about him that made him want to know so badly?

Oliver supposed, being something of an underdog himself, he had a sympathy for those who seemed to be in similar circumstances—although in reality he and Seph were absolute chalk and cheese. He was an overcompensating people-pleaser and she was…not. But he still wanted to know what she thought about the brownie—and the note. Definitely the note.

And yet, nearly twenty-four hours after he'd tiptoed into her workshop, making sure not to snoop or touch anything—leaving it right by the door so she'd know he hadn't—he'd had not a word. Not even a glance.

And that was okay, Oliver told himself as he filed a paid invoice for roof slates from October of thirteen months ago in its appropriate folder. Because he hadn't given her the brownie—or even the note—to extract something from her, or make her feel she owed him something. At least, not *much*. It was hard to be completely noble and self-sacrificing, but he was trying. Sort of.

And so really, he shouldn't expect her to say anything at all. He should just be cool with having done the right thing, and move on, totally chill. Too bad that wasn't really his personality. Instead he was slotting papers into folders and obsessing about a woman who probably couldn't care less. Sadly.

"Oliver?"

He didn't recognise the hesitant, wavering voice at first, and then he blinked in surprise when he saw it was actually Seph herself standing in the doorway. She was wearing what he suspected, although he'd only known her for two days, was her usual sort of outfit—a very worn, unbuttoned plaid shirt over paint-splattered dungarees and a pair of badly scuffed work boots. Her pink dreadlocks were standing out in all directions, but the uncertain expression on her face wasn't one he'd ever seen before. It was the first time, he realised, that he'd seen her when she wasn't scowling or shouting or worse, and he realised with a jolt that went right through him: *she's beautiful.*

Some part of him had known that already, but now he

felt it right down to his bones. And other places.

Her skin was glowing and clear, her face heart shaped, her eyes aquamarine, her lips full and lush. And her body, beneath the baggy clothes, looked slender yet curvy in all the right places. Yes, he was definitely noticing. He yanked his gaze upwards.

"Um, Seph. Hey." He straightened, wincing at the ache in his lower back from, admittedly, less than an hour of stooping over a filing cabinet. How many hours would it take to finish? Althea was a sadist, or at least had some sadistic tendencies she probably needed to curb. "How are you?"

"Um, okay." She looked down at the floor, scuffing her boot along the slate surface, her shoulder hunching a little. "I just wanted to say, ah, thanks for the brownie. And, um, the apology in your note. I know I freaked out on you, and so I, ah, am sorry, too. For that. I shouldn't have overreacted the way I did. I just...am kind of a private person." This came out in a stilted, staccato confession that he suspected she'd rehearsed, and somehow that endeared her to him all the more. Heaven knew why he liked this prickly woman, but he did.

"That's okay," he said, and she looked up at him quickly, her eyes glinting under her messy fringe, her expression both searching and anxious. "I was pretty presumptuous. You had every right to freak out. Not," he added quickly, "that I think you were freaking out, per se. React, I suppose. Be annoyed. At me. Understandably." He was officially babbling. As usual.

"Well, whatever I did." She gave him a shy smile then, like the sun peeking out from behind a cloud. It made Oliver's heart feel like a balloon in his chest, swelling, floating. He realised he was grinning back.

"So," he blurted before he lost his nerve, "what about that coffee?"

The look on Seph's face would have been comical if it didn't sting quite so much. She looked horrified, trapped as if he'd just backed her into a corner, and maybe he had. Oliver tried to school his own expression into something more casual than what he was feeling. "I mean, just as a thank you," he continued, trying for an offhand manner, like it didn't matter to him either way, which really, it *shouldn't*. "I don't actually know anyone in this part of the world, and you're about my age..." He tried not to wince at how, well, *desperate* he sounded. Jeez. Why couldn't he ever quit while he was ahead?

"I'm twenty-three," Seph said, like a question.

"And I'm twenty-five."

"Rose is twenty-four. Have you met her yet?" He shook his head and Seph continued, "Well, I guess that's not surprising. She's just had twins. She's my brother Sam's...well, significant other, I guess, although I'm sure they'll get married pretty soon."

"Okay." He wasn't all that interested in Rose right now,

frankly, and they definitely didn't need to go through everyone else's ages or the number of their offspring. "Well?" he asked, and now he sounded cringingly hearty. "What about the coffee?"

✻

SEPH STARED AT the hopeful look on Oliver's face and wondered why he was trying so hard. Did he feel sorry for her, misfit that she so obviously was, even in her own family? Unlike him, with his tailored clothes and cut-glass vowels, his easy manner, his breezy confidence. Every time he spoke, she was reminded of how posh he was. Althea, Olivia, and Sam all had that upper-class accent, from years at boarding school, but it had missed her out because she'd never gone away to school. She had a Cumbrian twang more than anything else, and while it had never out-and-out embarrassed her before, she noticed it now.

She was different. She'd always been different.

"I know you're busy," he said after a moment, and she realised she'd just been staring.

"Sorry…I…I was thinking," she half-mumbled, flushing in embarrassment. He must think her absolutely batty.

"About having a coffee with me?" The smile he gave her was wry, whimsical, a quirk of his lip that revealed a dimple in his right cheek. His green eyes glinted from behind his glasses, and he stuck his hands in the pockets of his chinos, rocking back on his heels.

Could she have a coffee with this man? She'd been turning the question over since he'd asked it in his note, although she'd done her best to ignore him without seeming as if she was last night, because she wasn't ready to give him an answer. Coming here to offer an apology had felt like the most she could do, and, in all honesty, more than she normally would, and she'd half-convinced herself that he wouldn't repeat the invitation to go out for a coffee, because…well, he just wouldn't.

But now he had, and he needed an answer, an answer she should be able to give right off, because it was only coffee, after all. Why was she tying herself in knots about it? All right, it would, almost undoubtedly, be terribly awkward. Social chitchat was definitely not something she could do with any kind of skill or ease. But Seph felt she was completely out of excuses and the truth was, she realised, she sort of *wanted* to go out with him somewhere. Show him as well as herself that she could do these normal things and not have it be a big deal.

There wasn't any other reason she'd be agreeing, was there?

"Sure," she said, a bit too expansively, shrugging like she went out for coffee all the time. "Why not?"

Oliver blinked, and then smiled. "Great. How about this afternoon? As long as this filing doesn't take me the rest of the day, or really, my entire internship. I don't think your sister has filed a single paper, ever."

"She's too busy to do the boring stuff, I guess," Seph replied, and realised belatedly there had been a slight edge to her voice. She and Althea had had it out—a bit—when her older sister had come swanning back to Casterglass, ready to save the day even though Seph had been here all along, quietly working and keeping the place going, along with her parents. That hadn't seemed to count for much with Althea, but she had apologised—more or less—for being MIA for basically Seph's entire life. And Seph had—more or less—accepted that apology.

But some things still rankled. Downright hurt, if she was honest, although she tried not to feel it.

"It's good for the soul, I suppose," Oliver said after a pause, with a quick, light smile. "Humbling, anyway. So. Coffee. Where can you get the best cuppa?"

"The Village Bakery in Broughton is pretty good," Seph said, and Oliver beamed.

"That's where I got your brownie."

She blinked, surprised, gratified. "You went all the way to Broughton-in-Furness to get me a brownie?"

"Well..." Oliver grinned a bit shamefacedly, seeming embarrassed, although Seph thought maybe his hangdog manner had to be affected. He seemed too confident to actually be embarrassed about anything. "Yes. I was hoping Casterglass Village might have something, but..."

"They have a pub and a post office." She smiled back at him, genuinely touched that he'd gone to such trouble. She couldn't remember the last time someone had. "Thank you for going all that way."

"It wasn't any trouble. I enjoyed exploring the area. I didn't realise quite how remote Casterglass was, actually. Definitely the back of beyond."

She laughed even as she grimaced. "You've got that right."

Once again, her tone had a bit of an edge and Oliver looked as if he wanted to ask her a million questions, so Seph said hurriedly, "Anyway, this afternoon, yes. I need to finish up in the workshop, but I should be free by three. If that's not too late?"

"Three's perfect."

"Great." She gave him one last smile, uncertainty making its edges wobble, and then with a nod, she backed out of the room and hurried down the hallway, her head down so she nearly smacked right into Olivia.

"Goodness, you're in a hurry!" her sister exclaimed, laughing. "Is there a fire?"

"No." Seph realised she was blushing—as if she was embarrassed, or had something to hide, or both. Olivia's laughing expression immediately turned to something both concerned and shrewd.

"Everything all right, Seph?"

"Yes. Fine." Of all her siblings, Olivia had been the most involved when she'd been growing up—checking in periodically, asking her how she was. She'd had her over to York a couple of times, which had been fun if a bit daunting. Seph appreciated the effort she'd made, but she still had the sense that she'd disappeared completely from Olivia's mind as soon as she returned to Casterglass. The Sister Nobody Knew, that had been her. Still was.

Olivia peered closely at her. "Are you sure?"

"Yes, Olivia, of course I'm sure!" In her unease Seph did what she always did—turned snarky and sullen. "I just have a lot of work to do, unlike some people, it seems," she added, and hurried down the hallway before her sister could ask her any more questions.

Back in her shop she paced for a few minutes, walking off the excitement—and anxiety—of what was ahead.

"Get a grip," she said aloud, half-annoyed with her own freakery. "It's a *coffee*."

It wasn't as if she'd never gone out before. She did social-ise, on occasion. She and her friend Doug, a casual labourer at John's farm, had gone to the Casterglass pub plenty of times, and yet mainly it was to down a pint in silence, or play darts, also in silence. A get-to-know-you coffee with someone like Oliver, who seemed so sure of himself, had gone to Oxford, spoke like a proper posh person, had probably had loads of experiences, travelled to places she hadn't even heard of...well, that was outside of her realm of experience, and it made her nervous, and yes, excited too. A little.

Should she change? she wondered. Would that be too

obvious? Could she do anything with her hair, which she knew full well was ridiculous—half straight blonde, half pink dreadlocks? She'd decided to dye and dread her hair a year ago, as a kind of armour against the world, but when Althea had started getting the castle ready to open, she'd suggested, *somewhat* tactfully, that Seph try not to look so scary. She'd huffed at her sister's high-handed request, but the truth was she was tired of looking—and feeling—ferocious, and growing her hair out seemed like a relatively easy way to change her image.

Could she go further than that, though?

Not today, Seph decided. It was still a couple of hours before she had to meet Oliver, so she decided to focus on her work. When she had wood under her hands and the lathe purring along, her mind emptied out, a blissful feeling after the welter of emotions she'd been dealing with today, far more than she usually let herself.

Two hours later, however, as soon as she switched off the machine and wiped the sweat and sawdust from her face, the feelings all came rushing back. Excitement. Anxiety. Worry. Hope. Seph took a deep breath and decided she would change after all, since she was wearing old work clothes, and it felt like a reasonable thing to do. A clean pair of jeans, Converse sneakers instead of work boots, and a baggy sweater were hardly making too much of an effort, surely? She pulled her dreadlocks back into a ponytail, and after a second's hesitation slicked on some lip balm, which was the only make-up she ever used, not that it was really make-up. Still, she felt as if she had a painted face as, her heart hammering, she headed downstairs.

Oliver was waiting in the kitchen, jangling the keys in his pocket, as she came down the stairs. His face lit up as he saw her and somehow this made Seph smile. He'd cleaned up too, she saw, just a little—a new pair of pressed cords and yet another button-down shirt, this one in pale pink. Did the man wear anything else? He was as strait-laced as they came, she supposed. Why on earth did he want to have anything to do with her?

And yet he did, because his smile widened as he leapt to open the door.

"After you," he said graciously, and with a nod of thanks Seph headed outside.

Chapter Five

"SO," OLIVER ASKED as he opened the door of his battered VW, "what was it like, growing up at Casterglass?"

He'd meant it as an easy opener, but the startled, guarded look Seph gave him made him feel as if he'd asked something intrusive. This was either going to be a very long afternoon, he thought, or a depressingly short one. Hopefully he wouldn't put his foot in it too many times in his bungling attempts to get to know her.

"It was okay," she said after a moment as she climbed into the car, sounding as guarded as she'd looked.

"Your sisters seem quite a bit older than you," he remarked as he reversed and then started down the drive. "Were they around when you were growing up?"

She tensed, her shoulders scrunching practically all the way to her ears, and Oliver realised he must have asked another zinger. Well, were they supposed to talk about the weather? Actually, he reflected, maybe.

"No," she said after a moment, her face to the window.

"They weren't. They left for boarding school before I was born."

He hesitated, wondering if he should drop the subject, and then decided he wanted to know too much to do that, even if Seph was starting to sound pained. "Was that very hard?" he asked.

Another pause, her lips pressed together, her gaze on the heavy banks of drooping rhododendrons lining the drive. "It was lonely, sometimes."

Getting anything from her was like blood from a stone, Oliver reflected wryly. He half-wondered why he was even trying, even as he acknowledged he knew the answer. Because, for some contrary reason, he *liked* her. Was it just that she was a challenge, or something more? Or was he just falling into the depressingly familiar pattern of people-pleasing, needing everyone to like him? Regardless, he was going to try with Seph, and he decided a little honesty himself might help grease the conversational wheels.

"I had a bit of a lonely childhood myself," he told her as he turned onto the B road that wound its way through rolling hills, lush green even in November from all the rain, towards Broughton-in-Furness. "So I can relate, a little, although of course I don't want to presume anything."

She was silent for a few seconds, and then, finally, thankfully, she took his hint. "Why was your childhood lonely?"

"My mother left when I was five," he said, keeping his tone conversational out of a deeply ingrained sense of self-protection. There was honesty and then there was pathetical-ly milking the situation. He'd been explaining the rather bleak circumstances of his childhood to various people for nearly two decades, and he'd learned to treat it matter-of-factly, like it had never bothered him, which wasn't *miles* from the truth—not really. "I never knew my dad. Mum was a bit of a wanderer, wanted to see the world. She parked me with my uncle at Pembury Farm and then more or less never came back." He gave a little shrug to keep from seeming too self-pitying.

"Never?" Seph sounded both curious and appalled. "Not even once?"

"Well, not quite never," Oliver allowed, wishing he hadn't exaggerated for effect. Did he actually want her to feel sorry for him? No, surely not. "There were a few visits over the years." Visits that had been excruciating in their awk-wardness, and yet devastating in their impossible hope. Every time he'd ached for her to stay, but of course she never had. Eventually he'd learned to stop wanting such a thing. "She ended up moving out to Australia, settling in Brisbane. She's really happy there. We Skype sometimes, stuff like that." Very rarely, but still, he supposed it was something. He now regarded her as something along the lines of a casual ac-quaintance or distant cousin, but that was okay. It was better than nothing.

"She didn't want you to move out with her?" Seph asked.

Another shrug, for good measure. "I don't know if she

ever thought about that possibility seriously. By the time she'd settled down enough to consider it, I was in secondary school and my education would have been interrupted, so it was never even discussed."

"As if that's the worst thing," Seph interjected, her voice filled with sudden scorn. "I think I would have rather had my education interrupted, thanks."

Intrigued, Oliver remarked, "It sounds like you're speaking from personal experience."

"No, not really. I mean, I never had the option of moving anywhere. Casterglass has been it." She turned to look out the window and he glanced at her, strangely moved by the smooth curve of her cheek, the paleness of her skin, the tiny blonde hairs on the nape of her neck. When she wasn't scowling, there was something deeply and touchingly vulnerable about her. Or was that just his wishful thinking?

"What, then?" he asked, keeping his tone gentle.

She shrugged, just like he had. Her own form of self-protection? He had no idea how much he was projecting onto her. "I just think there are more important things," she replied, her tone sounding deliberately dismissive.

"Such as?"

"The usual. Family. Friends. Feeling..." she blew out a breath "...supported."

Which made him want to ask a million questions, but he decided to steer it back to his own experience, because he sensed she was getting pretty prickly. She'd folded her arms and jutted out her jaw, all the while still staring out the window as if her life depended on it.

"Well, that's why I stayed at Pembury, actually. I had a few friends at school, and I was pretty well settled, with my aunt and uncle." Even though that had, of course, had some downsides, especially after his aunt had moved to London. He didn't want to get into all of that now, however, not on top of the stuff with his mum. Seph would think he was really pathetic, then. "I don't think I would have been willing to go all the way to Australia," he said instead, "and start over living with a woman I barely knew, even if she was my mother."

"Do you ever wish you did?" she asked, finally turning to look at him, her eyes wide, her lips pursed, as if the question really mattered.

Oliver considered the idea. "No, I don't think so," he said at last, "because I love Pembury Farm."

Her lips twisted. "What about your aunt and uncle?"

"I love them too." Had he spoken a little too quickly? His relationship with his uncle Simon and aunt Penny was complicated, to say the least. And that wasn't without considering his cousin Jack.

"But you love the farm more." She sounded almost con-demning—or was he just feeling sensitive, because he'd mentioned the farm before he'd mentioned his relatives? He could tie himself in knots, wondering what was going on inside her head. It was so very hard to know.

"Not more, just… The way you love a place is different than the way you love a person, don't you think?"

"I don't know that it is." Her voice had turned hard, and she was looking out the window again.

"I wonder," Oliver remarked, trying to inject some humour into his voice to lighten the mood, "are we talking about Pembury or Casterglass?"

She turned to give him a swift, haughty look. "Pembury, of course," she replied, as if it were obvious. Maybe it had been.

"Your parents clearly love Casterglass," Oliver replied, deciding to press a little, just in case. "And you must, as well. Your whole family does. It almost feels like another person in your family."

She let out a hard huff of something that sounded almost like laughter before she gave a little shrug. "Yes, I suppose it is," she said, after a pause that made Oliver wonder.

"Do you love them in the same way?" he asked. "Your family and the place itself?"

"We weren't talking about me," she replied, and somehow that felt like the end of the conversation. They didn't talk any more after that, anyway. Seph continued staring out the window and Oliver could not think of another line of conversation innocuous enough without it sounding either feeble or forced.

Still, the silence that ensued the rest of the way to Broughton *almost* felt companionable, Oliver decided as he parked on the high street near the village bakery. It hadn't been tense, at least. Well, not *too* tense. He'd already realised getting to know Seph was going to be challenging, so he didn't feel particularly discouraged by her guarded answers. He was intrigued more than anything else, but also determined. A habit he had that had occasionally been to his own detriment, to be sure. *Stop being such a try-hard, Oliver. Why do you have to impress people so much? Are you so scared they won't like you?*

In the quiet of the car, he could hear his cousin's jeering voice before he made himself silence it.

"Right," he told Seph with a smile. "Time for a coffee."

❇

SHE WAS MAKING a mess of this, Seph knew full well. Oliver asking all those nosy questions…! It made her feel itchy inside, and she'd had to fight an urge to squirm in her seat all the way from Casterglass. Loving people and places…well, she certainly knew how much her parents loved Casterglass, but she hadn't wanted to get into it with Oliver. She'd either sound pathetic or bitter, and maybe she was both, but she could do her best not to seem it. Mentally she shook her head. Good grief, but she was hopeless. He was going to be seriously regretting asking her out for a coffee. She was seriously regretting it, already. Well, Seph amended as they headed into the bakery, sort of.

Because, she realised, as uncomfortable as Oliver's well-intentioned questions made her, there had been something invigorating about them, too. About someone trying to get to know her. Understand her. Yes, that was scary, very scary, but wasn't it what she'd wanted all along? For someone to care enough to ask? To listen?

"So what will we be having?" Oliver asked as they came up to the counter. "Latte, cappuccino, or a skinny soy double espresso with a shot of sugar-free vanilla?"

She rolled her eyes. "As if."

"What?" He widened his eyes innocently. "That's what I'm having."

She let out a surprised guffaw of laughter, making her blush and Oliver grin. "You are not."

"Well...I might settle for a straight Americano, but you know, they probably don't have sugar-free vanilla, anyway."

"Actually, we do." The lady behind the counter was smiling at them in a teasing way that made Seph think she believed them to be on a date. Instead of prickling at such a notion, however, she found herself relaxing into it. Why not let the lady think that? Anyway, maybe it was true. Sort of. A very little bit.

"I'll have a double-shot latte, please," she said firmly, and Oliver ordered an Americano before insisting on buying an enormous slice of Victoria sponge and a flapjack nearly the size of an electronic tablet as well.

"You can't have coffee without cake," he stated, as if it were a law written in stone, and they took their cups and plates to a table in the corner, by the window overlooking the street.

"So." He plunged right in, giving her a direct look as he speared a large forkful of cake. "Tell me something about yourself that no one else knows."

Seph nearly choked on her latte. That, she thought, was a horrifying prospect. "What…!"

He shrugged as he chewed and then swallowed his bite of cake. "It doesn't have to be a big thing. No deep secrets if you don't want to."

She shook her head slowly, reluctant to part with any information even as she searched for some innocuous fact to offer him.

"I'll go first, if you like," he said. "I came down with chicken pox three times."

"What!" She shook her head again. "That's impossible."

"Nope. Doctors confirmed it. Very rare, but it happened. All mild cases, fortunately. Fairly inconvenient, though. The last time I was nineteen. Spots all over my face. Awkward."

She smiled a little at that. "Hmm." She could, Seph thought, probably find a similarly innocent anecdote about childhood diseases or the like, if she tried. "I missed three months of school," she finally told him, "because I came down with the measles."

"The measles!" Oliver looked surprised. "You weren't vaccinated?"

Maybe not so innocuous, then, Seph realised with a lurch of alarm. She'd forgotten about the whole vaccination thing. "No, I didn't have any vaccinations until I was twelve."

"None? Why not?"

She took a sip of her coffee, her gaze sliding away. Oliver's mum had dumped him on his uncle's doorstep, she reminded herself, and he'd seemed surprisingly blasé about it. So she could be the same about this. "My parents forgot, actually. About them." *About me.*

Oliver's forehead furrowed. "Forgot?"

"Yep." She shrugged, forgetting that she was holding her coffee, and nearly spilled it. Quickly she put it back down on the table. "I was a serious afterthought—my brother Sam is ten years older than me, and Althea is nine years older than him. And you've met my parents—you know how, well, batty they are?"

"Charmingly so, but yes, I suppose." The smile Oliver gave her was tinged with compassion, and that made Seph look away quickly.

"Well, when I came along, they'd pretty much got out of the whole parenting groove, although to tell the truth I don't know how much they were ever truly in it. Stuff like vaccinations and toddler groups went by the wayside." She shrugged, this time thankfully without holding a scaldingly hot cup of coffee. "It was fine. I did my own thing. I liked it that way."

"What, as a baby?" Oliver was clearly joking but he had no idea how close to the truth he really was.

"Well, no, obviously not when I was an actual infant, but I grew up mostly on my own. They sent me to school for year six, the way they did with the others—we were all homeschooled before then." Although Seph had actually had precious little homeschooling; there had been occasional lessons when a particular interest had suddenly seized her mother, but beyond that she'd been left to her own devices.

"And year six was when you missed so much school because of the measles?"

He'd made that leap pretty quickly. The whole year had been a complete washout; she hadn't made any friends, and she'd been way behind in her work. "Yes, it turned into pneumonia, unfortunately." Oliver was frowning now, and it made Seph hasten to add, "It all turned out fine, honestly. I didn't even like school, so I was glad not to go. Big relief, really."

"Why didn't you like school?"

"I suppose because I wasn't used to it." And she'd been the weird kid, too weird even to be bullied. She'd been ignored instead; she suspected the other children simply hadn't known what to do with her. Which had been both a relief and a disappointment, really.

"So where did you go for secondary school?" Oliver asked, his forehead still furrowed.

"I stayed at home." She was going to sound like such an oddball now, Seph thought despondently, although he was probably thinking, *Ah, that makes sense. No wonder she's so strange.* That possibility made her feel even worse. "There wasn't enough money for boarding school by then, and I wasn't particularly keen on the local school, so I more or less homeschooled myself." Which had been *fine.* Kind of.

"Homeschooled yourself!" Oliver raised his eyebrows, his tone somewhere between impressed and scandalised. "How did you manage that?"

Seph hesitated, unsure whether to backpedal or brag. "I don't know. I just did."

"Oh, come on." Oliver leaned forward, his face alight. "You can't leave it at that. Did you take your GCSEs? Your A levels? I mean, what did you *do?*"

Seph felt herself flushing. "I took my GCSEs," she answered slowly. She'd registered for them online, ordered the books, taught herself. Occasionally her mother had fluttered by to see how she was doing, or her father would take a kindly interest and read one of her essays, but it had all felt very token; as if they'd completely forgotten about her and then suddenly remembered, *Oh right, we have another daughter. Should make a bit of an effort, perhaps!*

"And then I went to sixth form for my A levels," she finished, "but I didn't manage to actually get any." She buried her nose in her coffee cup then, unwilling—or perhaps unable—to meet his gaze. Would he be horrified? Pitying? Which would be worse?

"Why not?" Oliver asked after a moment. His tone was quiet, but she couldn't tell much from it.

She put her coffee cup down and broke off a bit of flapjack, crumbling it between her fingers. "I don't know. It just wasn't for me. I quit after year twelve." She risked a look up; his expression was alert without being too pitying. She hoped. "I guess you can't start school at sixth form without being seen as a little—weird."

Unlike in primary, the kids in sixth form had bullied her, in a careless sort of way. *Oh look, here comes that freak girl*, they might say as she came down the corridor. Looking back, Seph wasn't sure what had been so weird about her. All right, her social skills hadn't been amazing, and she'd been pretty sullen and silent. She'd also gone through a defiant Goth phase because, like the pink dreadlocks, black hair and lots of liquid eyeliner had felt like armour. But it hadn't felt like anything *too* out of the ordinary, except, for the back of beyond part of Cumbria, maybe it had been. Or maybe she really was weird, on some sort of fundamental level, because she found conversations like this one so difficult.

She tried to smile, but to her horror her lips were trembling. *Oh, help.* She hadn't meant to admit that much, she realised. *Reveal* it, because she felt so vulnerable and so, well, *sad.* She thought of her seventeen-year-old self, angry and defiant and so very afraid, and she ached for that girl. She wanted a do-over, but she also wanted to give herself a hug. Which was sort of ridiculous, because she didn't think she'd actually progressed all that much. Except here she was, talking about it with a nice—and cute—guy, so maybe she had, after all. At least a little.

The thought gave her enough strength to smile, even if her lips still trembled. "I'm not saying it wasn't hard, though," she said, in a tone that was meant to be wry but shook a little.

"It must have been really hard. I can't even imagine, and my own secondary school experience was somewhat unorthodox."

"Was it?"

He shrugged, the movement dismissive. "Not like yours. Not even close."

"Tell me." She craved some kind of shared experience, she realised, because it was something she hardly ever had. She'd been a loner for so much of her life, she didn't really know what it felt like, to say, *Yes, me too!* And yet she wanted to. Badly. She wanted that, she realised, with Oliver in particular.

He hesitated, his long, lean fingers toying with the handle of his coffee cup as his expression turned pensive. "Oh, I don't know," he said at last. "I just suppose I never really felt like I fit in, either. When my aunt and uncle took me in— well, they were really kind, but...I also felt...*other*. They sent their son Jack to this posh boarding school that my uncle had gone to, the kind of place where you wore a fancy uniform, complete with straw boater or what have you, and I went to the local comp. Not that I minded," he added quickly, leaning forward as if he really wanted her to understand. To believe him. "I didn't even want to go to that snooty school. But it just felt…" He shrugged, helplessly. "It felt like some sort of snub, even if it wasn't. Like I didn't matter quite as much, and why should I? I was the nephew, not the son. I suppose I was always aware of that, on some level. Sometimes more than at other times, but there was always something there."

"Yes." Seph felt a lump forming in her throat, because she understood *exactly* what he meant, how he'd felt. Hadn't she felt the same way? Like a forgotten addendum, the epilogue to their family that nobody had remembered to read. She'd never imagined that someone might feel similarly. Someone like Oliver, who seemed so posh and confident and relaxed.

She stared at him as if seeing him for the first time, not as someone she had to protect herself against, but someone who might actually understand her. Be her friend. Could it be possible?

Or was she just wishing it was? Heaven knew she had trouble trusting herself but as Oliver smiled at her and she smiled shyly back, she knew she wanted to. A lot.

Chapter Six

THEY WERE SMILING at each other like a pair of fools and Oliver liked it. He found he didn't want to break Seph's gaze, even though his eyes were beginning to water. He hadn't expected her to share so much, and he was glad she had, because he was starting to understand her so much better.

And he'd thought *he'd* had an unorthodox childhood! Seph clearly won that prize. He couldn't even imagine what it must have been like, to feel so, well, *forgotten*. He suspected she'd tried to downplay it a bit, so he wouldn't feel too sorry for her—hadn't he done the same thing? What a pair they were. *What a pair*. He found he liked that thought.

"And what about now?" he asked. "Now that everyone has come back? Do you like having a full house—or should I say castle—again?"

"I don't know if it's 'again' for me," Seph replied after a moment. "We never really had it before, at least not during my lifetime."

"Didn't everyone come back for holidays?"

"Sometimes, but Sam was often travelling, and Althea was married to this rotter, Jasper—they got divorced last year—who didn't like coming up here. So, the family get-togethers were pretty few and far between, to be honest." She crumbled off a bit of flapjack and popped it into her mouth. "I didn't mind too much. I've always been a solitary person."

She'd had to be, and so she'd learned to like it, Oliver surmised. "Needs must, I suppose," he replied. He sat back in his chair as he gazed at her, considering. There was a spark of defiance in her blue-green eyes, as well as a shadow of vulnerability. Her arms were folded, her chin tilted—ready to take on the world, or hide from it? Maybe both.

"What about you?" she asked. "Are you close to your aunt and uncle? You said you always felt like the nephew. What did you mean, exactly?"

The questions came thick and fast, with a hint of challenge. Oliver took a sip of his coffee, mainly to stall for time. Seph had been pretty honest in her answers, even if he suspected she'd tried to keep stuff back. He supposed he could, too.

"My cousin Jack has always been one of those sporty blokes," he said slowly, "if you know what I mean. First eleven this, first eleven that, rugby all through secondary and then rowed all through university in his college's first boat, at Oxford." In case he was sounding spiteful, as if this was nothing but envy, he added quickly, "And, I mean, good for him, absolutely. But he didn't have much time for me."

Seph's eyes narrowed as she cocked her head. "Was he a bully?"

"Not as such," Oliver replied carefully. Jack had never hit him; he hadn't had to, because Oliver had cowered beneath his cousin's scorn anyway. "He just always let me know he was better than me, I suppose, and my uncle did, as well. I mean there was no question—I couldn't compete, not even a tiny bit. He was the captain of the rugby team; I was a geek."

Seph's eyebrows rose in surprise. "A geek?" she repeated. "You don't seem like a geek to me."

He laughed, clasping one hand to his heart. "Words to treasure. Trust me, I was—I was five foot four until I was seventeen, and then I had a massive growth spurt. Someone mistook me for a year seven in sixth form. Ouch."

She let out a soft laugh and he grinned, glad he could joke about it now. It had been pretty hard at the time, especially with Jack a strapping six two, swanning home from his boarding school with his posh friends while Oliver had been slinking back from the comp, alone.

"What about Pembury Farm?" Seph asked abruptly, and he could tell from her narrowed expression exactly what she was thinking. "If things were the way you've said, surely your cousin will inherit it?"

"Ah." Oliver took the last forkful of Victoria sponge, chewing slowly and swallowing before he answered. "Well, he would, and that was my uncle's great hope, of course. But Jack has zero interest in living at Pembury—it's not as remote as Casterglass, but it's in the North Yorkshire Moors and it feels quite rural. He lives in London, works as a banker in the City. He wants my uncle to sell it, since it's his inheritance. He'd rather have a million pounds or so, free and clear, than a draughty old house up in the moors, definitely."

"And you want your uncle to keep it," she said, a statement.

"Yes." Oliver heard the throb of passion in his voice and smiled, abashed by his own emotion. "I do. I love Pembury Farm. It's the only home I've known—like Casterglass is to you."

Seph raised her eyebrows, saying nothing, and Oliver continued, "I'm sure we could make it a going concern. It wouldn't give Jack a million pounds, it's true, but it could provide a stable income of sorts."

And now she was shaking her head. "But he'll inherit it anyway, won't he? Even if your uncle agrees to let you run it for a time? It'll be his in the long run."

"Ye-es." He rotated his empty coffee cup between his hands, the reality of his circumstances depressing him yet again. Was he crazy, to think he could change his uncle's mind? "My hope is that I could buy Jack out, in time. If he agreed. All he wants is the money, so it's not impossible. If I had the money, I mean." Although virtually impossible, Oliver acknowledged, especially if his uncle didn't leave him anything in his will, which he doubted he would; it probably wouldn't even occur to his uncle. All Oliver wanted was the farm, but it still felt like too much.

He pictured the place now—its weathered stone and smoke-stained beams, the huge fireplace in the low-ceilinged living room, the rumbling Rayburn in the kitchen, with the dried herbs dangling from the beams, the long refectory table where he'd had almost every meal of his childhood. He thought of the rolling hills, the twisted, knobbly apple trees, the big stone barn that still smelled of hay and animals even though they hadn't kept horses in twenty years. He loved every inch of that place, had found solace in its quiet corners, in roaming its meadows and fields. His uncle knew that; he knew Pembury was in Oliver's blood, his very bones. How could he sell it, just to give Jack, who was already raking it in, a bit more dosh?

"I admit, it's not a dead cert," he said with a rallying sort of smile. "But I've got to try. I asked my uncle if I could try to turn the place into a going concern, but he said I didn't have any experience. I asked him if he would consider the matter if I gained some experience, and he said yes. So here I am."

"You must really love that place," Seph said slowly. There was a faraway, wistful look to her face.

"Yes, I do, just like you love Casterglass, I think." He smiled, but the glance she gave him was strangely sharp. "I mean, you stayed," he said, with a hint of a question in his voice.

"Yes," she agreed. "I stayed." She glanced at the chunky watch strapped to her wrist in a deliberate sort of way. "It's nearly five. We should get back."

"All right," Oliver replied, even though he wanted to ask *why?* He'd been having such a good time. He thought Seph had too, until something he'd said seemed to have spoiled it, just a little.

"Thank you for the coffee." The words were formal as she rose from the table. "It was very kind of you."

"It was my pleasure." He hesitated and then added, a bit recklessly, "I've enjoyed getting to know you. I hope to have the opportunity to get to know you more, over the next three months."

Seph's cheeks went pink as she looked away. "I'm not sure how much more there is to get to know," she replied, which Oliver thought was disingenuous. Surely he'd barely scratched the surface.

Outside it had already gone dark, the village cloaked in blackness as he went around to open the passenger door for her. She mumbled something about him not needing to, before offering a belated thanks, and then they were driving through the village, even quieter now that the sun had set, through fells that were no more than humps in the darkness, back to Casterglass.

Oliver was uncomfortably aware that he'd scarpered off for most of the afternoon, having left Althea only a note. At least he'd done all the filing. Still, it wasn't the best look, to disappear on only your second day of work. So, while Seph headed to her workshop, he went to beard Althea in her den.

"Oliver, this is marvellous!" she exclaimed as he came into the little office. "You've done it all—I thought it would take you days. You are remarkably efficient."

"Well." He shrugged modestly, relieved she wasn't annoyed he'd taken off for the end of the afternoon. Besides, filing wasn't exactly rocket science, was it?

"Right, what next? At this rate you'll have the whole place in shape before Christmas."

"I thought perhaps I could sort the orchard out?" Oliver suggested, a bit hesitant to offer his own ideas to the fearsome Althea. "I know I can't prune the trees until winter, but I could clear the nettles and brambles out while they've died down, I think? Make it ready for spring?" He'd learned that last part from YouTube.

"That sounds like a wonderful project," Althea replied, "but don't you want experience in all the areas?"

"Yes—" He'd also wanted something he could think of as his own, something he could show his uncle that he'd done alone, but perhaps he was being presumptuous.

"I know," Althea suggested, "why don't you work on the orchard in the mornings, and in the afternoons, you could look into developing it online?" Althea's face was alight with the idea. "We'd need to add it onto our website, do the marketing, run the numbers to see if it's feasible to run pick-your-own. Or cider making, perhaps?" She threw her arms wide. "The world's your oyster, or at least the orchard is."

Oliver's stomach flared with excitement. Handling a project like that would surely impress his uncle, more than filing papers or tinkering with a spreadsheet, anyway. He could show him how he'd managed it from start to finish, and how it could work at Pembury. It would be brilliant. Well, it could be. Maybe.

"That would be amazing, Althea," he said. "Thank you."

"Trust me, you're the one who is doing me a favour, not the other way around," she replied. "Now, you know about tomorrow night?"

He tried not to look too blank. "Tomorrow night?"

"We're having a trial run of one of our proposed winter evenings—sherry, mince pies, that sort of thing, for all the locals. If it works, we'll offer them once a week. I'd love to hear your ideas about the whole concept, of course, but if you could help serve tomorrow night, that would be wonderful."

Serve mince pies? So he went from project manager of Casterglass Orchards to being a waiter at a family party? Oliver swallowed down any twinge of resentment he felt, because he knew it wasn't really about tomorrow night. He was remembering all the family occasions he'd been relegated to a similar status—staying home to watch his aunt's dogs, who apparently couldn't be left alone, while they went out for Jack's birthday dinner. Christmases where Jack opened a dozen presents and Oliver had one. All right, he hadn't actually been counting, he didn't even care, but he'd still *felt* it. In a thousand little ways, each one making him feel bitter, and then petty for feeling so.

"Oliver? Will that be okay?" Althea's tone had turned the tiniest bit strident.

"Sure, of course," he said quickly, smiling easily, as always. "Absolutely no problem at all. I'll love it." Okay, that was definitely a bit much. He knew he was not going to love it.

"Great." She looked relieved, and with a smile Oliver excused himself. He knew he didn't really mind about serving at the party. It was just little things like that brought up all the old resentment that he tried to forget, that he didn't want to feel, because then it made him wonder how on earth he might ever be allowed to keep hold of Pembury Farm.

If Jack found out what he was hoping for, he'd probably be furious, or scornful, or both. *As if you'd ever get Pembury*, he'd tell Oliver, laughing at the sheer absurdity of it. Maybe his uncle was laughing at him. Maybe he'd suggested Oliver get some experience just as a way to fob him off. It wasn't the first time he'd wondered such a thing, and it made him feel deeply depressed. If this was all nothing more than a futile fool's errand, utterly hopeless...

But at least, he told himself, he'd met Seph. Not that he was expecting it to go anywhere, not that he even wanted it to, but he really had enjoyed getting to know her. He'd meant what he said about getting to know her more—because there definitely was more to get to know, no matter what she'd said, and he really hoped she'd let him find out.

Chapter Seven

"YOU CAN'T WEAR that."

Olivia stood in the doorway of Seph's bedroom, her hands on her hips, her expression caught between laughter and horror.

"What?" Seph demanded, reverting to sullenness, as usual. Some habits were hard to break. She glanced down at her baggy jeans and loose jumper. "This is fine."

"Seph, this is meant to be something of a special occasion," Olivia said, a hint of laughter in her voice. "Those jeans look like you fished them out of a charity bin. You really should wear a dress, or at least a pair of tailored trousers." She pursed her lips, eyeing her critically, making Seph fidget.

"I don't own a dress," she told Olivia. "And I'd look ridiculous in one, anyway." She did not do dress up. Ever.

"You wouldn't, you know." Olivia's tone gentled. "You've got a knockout figure, and you should show it off, at least a little."

"I don't want to." She had never, ever wanted to draw

attention to herself, which she supposed was a bit ironic, considering how much she had always craved someone to notice her. To care. The human heart was a mass of contradictions, Seph supposed with an inward sigh. At least hers was. It was twenty-four hours since her coffee with Oliver, and she hadn't seen him once since, something that had both disappointed and relieved her—as usual. She hadn't known what she would say when she saw him, but she realised she'd wanted the chance to say *something*. When, after he'd missed lunch, she'd asked Althea what he was doing, in the most offhand manner she could manage, her sister had immediately looked beady.

"He's up working in the orchard. Why?"

Seph had shrugged, immediately defensive. "Just curious. He was nosing around in my workshop, and I wanted to make sure he stayed away." She'd instantly regretted saying such a thing, feeling weirdly disloyal to Oliver, and was grateful he couldn't hear her.

"I told him he could nose around the place, get a feel for things," Althea replied with a shrug. "Don't be so touchy, Seph. He's working hard."

Seph had had to bite her lip to keep from issuing a sharp retort, and then she marched off to her workshop, bristling with indignation. Now it was late afternoon, and everyone was getting ready for this winter thing they were holding in the grand entrance hall of the castle. Seph hadn't had anything to do with the planning, but Althea had some idea of a trial run of some sort of party, with drinks and nibbles. They were inviting neighbours and friends, with the idea that if it was successful, they could hold them once a week through December, offering a candlelit tour of the castle to boot. Seph hadn't even been planning to show up, but then Althea had put her foot down and said every Penryn had to be present.

Normally Seph would have ignored such a diktat, but this time she hadn't, and she knew why. She wanted to see Oliver again. But not while wearing a dress.

"Could you at least try one on?" Olivia pleaded. "For my sake."

"What's the big deal? It's just going to be a bunch of nosy old villagers there, anyway, snooping around the castle." Most of the people her age had left Casterglass for the wider world, whether that was only as far as Kendal or all the way to London. They didn't stick around here the way she had, at any rate.

"Still," Olivia pressed. "I'd like you to do it for your sake, not the villagers'. Don't you want to look pretty?"

"No."

Her sister rolled her eyes. "Come on, Seph. Not even a little? I'm not talking ball gown and stilettos here. Just a simple, easy, nice dress."

"How can a dress be easy?"

Olivia let out a sound that was half-laugh, half-groan. "Come *on*. Let's at least look at what I have. I think we're about the same size."

Seph hesitated; normally she would say an absolute no to something like this and that would be the end of it. Although, she acknowledged, normally no one would suggest such a thing, either because they knew not to or they simply didn't care. But Olivia was caring enough to take an interest, and Oliver's interest in her had given Seph the tiniest flicker of vanity, so she didn't want to be clomping around in her dungarees and work boots while everyone was else was floating around in velvet or silk.

"All right," she relented. "I'll look. But no promises."

"Of course not," Olivia said on a laugh, and then she tugged on Seph's hand to lead her to her bedroom down the hall.

Seph perched uneasily on the edge of Olivia's bed while she riffled through her wardrobe, a cavernous thing of ancient mahogany that was big enough to hold a body or three. Outside the night was already drawing in, and fairy lights lined the winding drive, twinkling with welcome in the dusk. Althea really had thought of everything, Seph acknowledged, and she worked hard, as bossy as she could be.

"What about this?"

Olivia held out a red velvet number, far too slinky for Seph's taste.

"No."

"This?"

A little LBD that wouldn't even cover her knees. "No."

"Seph, these are reasonable suggestions!" Olivia protested. "Couldn't you at least try them on?"

"No."

She wasn't actually trying to be difficult, even if Olivia thought she was. She simply had a horror of making an effort and then being laughed at, made to feel weird, the way she had in school. Better not to try. Not to care.

"This one?" Olivia asked hopefully, holding out a wrap dress in soft green wool, the colour of moss, with tiny, shimmering threads of blue and brown running through it. Seph hesitated, and Olivia jumped on that second's pause. "Yes," she said firmly. "This is the one. It's perfect for you."

Slowly, reluctantly yet with a tiny, treacherous bit of excitement, Seph rose from the bed. "I'll look like some sort of woodland elf."

"And that is totally a look," Olivia replied swiftly. "Cottagecore meets Goth fantasy."

"There is nothing Goth about this dress."

"Pair it with some knee-high leather boots. You'll look amazing."

Seph shook her head doubtfully, but she took the dress. She'd try it on, and when she proved to Olivia that she did look ridiculous in a dress, as she'd always known, she'd take it off again. And go to the party in jeans and boots, as usual.

Why did that thought depress her, just a little?

Because you want to be different than you usually are. You want to be like everyone else for once.

"Look the other way," she commanded and, rolling her eyes, Olivia turned her back while Seph swiftly undressed and slipped the dress on. The wool whispered softly against her skin, the dress fitting far more snugly than anything she'd ever worn. Apprehensively, she glanced in the mirror, while Olivia's back was still turned.

She'd barely taken in her reflection when Olivia let out a little shriek. "Oh, Seph! You look stunning! You could be a model, you know, with that figure. Your waist is *tiny.*"

Seph put her hands to her waist, amazed at how the dress nipped it in and then flared out from her hips, to swirl about her calves. She'd never, ever worn something like this. She looked like a completely different person. She *felt* like a completely different person. Well, almost.

"I don't know…" she began, alarmed as well as intrigued by this new vision of herself. She'd wanted to look like everyone else, but she hadn't realised just how different she would look. How everyone would be bound to notice.

"You've got to wear it," Olivia commanded. "I'm not letting you take it off."

"It feels like too much."

"Too much?" Olivia let out a snort of laughter. "Our mother is going to be wearing a silk muumuu, and Dad is bringing out his old velvet smoking jacket, complete with matching bow tie. I'm amazed the moths haven't got that thing yet. You'll be casual in comparison, trust me. But I don't think we can go with boots, after all. I've got a pair of heels…" She hurried over to the wardrobe to rummage in its bottom.

"Heels!" Seph couldn't keep from sounding horrified. "I've never worn heels. I'll trip in them. I'll break my ankle." *I'll look ridiculous.*

"We'll practise," Olivia assured her. "Here they are." She withdrew a pair of low black heels that didn't look *too* daunting. Still Seph felt hesitant.

"I don't want to look as if I'm trying too hard," she said, biting her lip, knowing already that she would.

"Why not?" Olivia asked baldly. "What's the big deal? We should all try a bit sometimes." A knowing gleam came into her eyes, making Seph tense. "Is there someone in particular you're wanting to impress without seeming like you are?" she asked in a teasing voice.

"No, of course not," Seph scoffed. She felt herself begin to blush and she grabbed the heels. "Fine. I'll try them."

It took over twenty minutes of practising before Seph could walk in the heels without wobbling all over the place, and even then she was tottering carefully, as if she were walking on her tiptoes across splintering ice.

"I can't do this," she declared, exasperated, as she flung off one shoe. "High heels are stupid."

"Amen to that," Olivia agreed. "We'll find you some flats if you're really struggling. But let's think about your hair and make-up—"

"No," Seph said quickly. "No make-up."

"A little bit of lip gloss," she begged. "And a flick of eye-liner. That's all."

"No, absolutely not." Seph was adamant. "I look like a clown when I wear even lip balm. Forget it."

Olivia let out a gusty sigh. "All right, fine. But what about your hair?"

Seph touched her dreadlocks self-consciously. "What about it?"

"Maybe it's time to cut the dreads," Olivia suggested. "Your hair has grown out a bit. You'd look amazing with a cute pixie cut."

Seph hesitated, glancing in the mirror. Her once hot pink dreadlocks had faded to the colour of pink-tinged dishwater, and they were looking decidedly unkempt. She was ready to be rid of them, and yet she feared she'd feel naked without their protection. They'd been a shield between her and the world, a way to seem tough and declare 'keep away.'

But maybe she didn't want to seem or say that anymore, at least not quite so vehemently.

"It's past four," she finally said. "I won't be able to get a hair appointment. And I'm not having you cut them." She wagged a warning finger at her sister. There was a family story of Olivia cutting Sam's hair so jaggedly he'd had to have a buzz cut at three years old.

"I wouldn't dream of it," Olivia promised her. "But Helen down in the village has a mobile hair salon… I could give her a quick text, tell her it's an absolute emergency?"

"It's not an emergency," Seph protested, but part of her was already treacherously warming to the idea. In this dress and a pair of nice flats, with her hair cut and maybe a tiny bit of lip gloss, she'd look like everybody else. She'd fit in, for once.

But what if you still don't?

That would be worse, she knew, than never fitting in at all. "I don't think—" she began, only for Olivia to hold up her phone in triumph.

"I just texted her and she's already replied. She can be here in fifteen minutes."

"What!" Seph stared at her sister, panic beginning to pool in her stomach as the reality of it all hit her smack in the face. She really was trying too hard, and absolutely everyone would know, because she never did. She never tried at all. "Olivia, no. I don't want to go to all this effort." She kicked off the heels, fighting a proper panic now. "I'll just wear my jeans and boots. No one will notice me, anyway—"

"Seph." Olivia placed her hands on her shoulders to still her, her voice gentle. "What exactly are you afraid of?"

"I'm not *afraid*—" Seph almost snarled.

"Come on. I know you. You're freaking out over wearing a dress and getting your hair cut. It doesn't have to be a big deal, you know."

Seph shrugged her sister's hands away. "But I never do

this stuff," she half-mumbled. "And everyone will notice and comment on it. 'Oh, Seph, really putting the boat out tonight! Who are you trying to impress, then?'" She could practically hear Althea trumpeting such a statement while everyone listened in, smirking. The thought alone was nearly enough to have her breaking out in hives.

"Okay, so then you just tell them you felt like a change. Shrug it off, or bite their head off if you'd rather, like you normally do. Who cares? This is for you, Seph, not them." Olivia's expression softened along with her voice. "Don't hide yourself away. You don't need to."

Seph blinked, appalled to realise she actually had tears in her eyes, from her sister's gentle words. She twisted away so Olivia wouldn't see. She'd hidden away all her life, she thought, in one way or another. Stuck here at Casterglass, forgotten by just about everyone…she'd made hiding her choice, whether it was by being invisible or seeming too tough to care. At least it had given her the illusion of feeling in control.

"You can do this," Olivia said quietly. "But only if you want to. I won't force you—"

"Really?" Seph couldn't keep from retorting. "Because that's what you've been doing all afternoon."

"Well, I'll stop right now. This has to be your decision. Your desire." Olivia stepped back, flinging her hands wide. "It's up to you, Seph."

Just then a voice floated up the stairs. "Hello, Olivia? It's

Helen, the mobile hairdresser…"

Seph met Olivia's laughing gaze as her sister bit her lip, clearly unrepentant. "Whoops. Well, I *could* send her away…"

Seph glanced back at the mirror. She *did* look good in this dress, she thought with a sudden, fierce surge of determination. And screw anyone who thought differently! She'd bite their head off, just like Olivia said. Why not? If she could do it in dungarees and boots, she could do it in a dress. She threw back her shoulders, lifted her chin.

"Fine," she told Olivia. "Let's do this."

❄

OLIVER WAS SKULKING. Walter Penryn had cornered him in the kitchen while he'd been loading up a tray with canapés and had insisted, with a sense of great beneficence and ceremony, that Oliver wear his great-grandfather's velvet smoking jacket for the party that evening. Oliver would have been perfectly content in his usual uniform of button-down shirt and cords; for the occasion he'd ironed his shirt and added a very small spritz of aftershave.

Unfortunately, Walter wasn't taking no for an answer, and so Oliver found himself crammed into a very worn jacket in emerald-green velvet with black silk lapels that smelled like mothballs and strained uncomfortably across his shoulders, while hefting a tray of smoked salmon on mini toasts. To say he felt ridiculous was, sadly, a gross understatement.

Althea had actually snorted when she'd seen him. "My father must really like you," she'd remarked, which had caused Oliver to smile weakly. Heaven help him if her father started to *dis*like him, he thought, although perhaps that would be a relief. He wouldn't have to wear this jacket, anyway.

He'd been so busy with the orchard that he hadn't seen Seph since their coffee, and he was eager to see her again, to make sure they were still friendly. He had a horrible suspicion that she might revert back to her sullen self, and he really didn't want that. They'd actually been *getting* somewhere, out at the bakery, and Oliver did not want to lose ground. He'd meant to come back to the castle for lunch, just to check in, but he'd been waist-deep in brambles, hacking things with a scythe and working up a sweat, and that had felt good.

He liked feeling like he was accomplishing something, like he was, in a very small way, king of his own castle, or at least his own orchard. And he hoped, when his uncle saw what he'd done, he'd be impressed enough to hand him the keys to Pembury Farm.

Who are you kidding?

Now, standing by the front door while guests began to trickle in, Oliver did his best to silence that voice—and look for Seph.

The hall was filling up, various locals snatching up glasses of champagne or rum punch, helping themselves to the canapés Oliver offered, while mingling in front of the roaring fire, chatting and laughing. Althea had roped her thirteen-year-old son Tobias in as well as Oliver to pass around trays of nibbles, so at least he wasn't the only one on waiter duty. Olivia had arranged vases of winter jasmine and Christmas roses around that gave off a lovely, festive scent, even though it was only November, and really, it all looked very cosy and welcoming.

It was a beautiful home, Oliver thought, far grander than Pembury, yet with a lovable, lived-in shabbiness to it that made him feel comfortable. He wondered if Pembury's reception rooms were big enough to cater events, and then decided that they probably weren't. But maybe, he mused, he could turn the old stone barn into some sort of reception hall. Swept out, with a chandelier above perhaps, space for a country band, it could be ideal for rustic weddings...

He was so lost in his thoughts that he almost missed her. She had inched into the hall, looking more wary than sullen, and it took him several blinks to recognise her. Was that *Seph*?

She'd got rid of her dreadlocks, he noticed first off, and her hair fell about her face in short, messy blonde ringlets. His gaze moved down and then widened at the sight of her in a dress—an actual dress. And what a dress it was, bringing out the green in her eyes, clinging to her willowy figure before flaring out about her long, slender legs... He choked on a laugh as he saw then what she was wearing on her feet—her old, clumpy work boots, and yet somehow, with her, the whole ensemble worked. He was glad she was wearing those boots, he realised, almost fiercely. He was glad she was who she was, boots and all.

He took a step towards her, a sloppy grin already spreading across his face, ready to make a joke about his own dubious outfit, when he stopped, because Sam had paused to speak to her.

"Wow, look at you, Seph," Sam said, whistling softly. "Who are you trying to impress?"

Her shy smile immediately morphed into a scowl. "No one."

"Are you sure about that?" Sam teased, and Seph's scowl deepened so there were deep grooves on either side of her frowning mouth. "Althea told me you seemed into that guy who has come here to intern. Oscar? Oliver?"

"I'm not *into* him," she declared shortly while Oliver stood there, lurking in the shadows, tray of canapés suspended, transfixed and horrified.

"Well, I certainly haven't ever seen you in a dress before," Sam replied with a laugh. "So you must be scrubbing up for someone. It's all right to have a crush, you know." Oliver thought he meant well, but the careless remarks would, he already knew, be like acid on a wound to Seph. Why, he wondered, could he understand that better than her family seemed to?

Because he knew how it felt—that careless teasing, indifferent to the pain caused, never really understanding what made the other person tick—or bleed. That was how his aunt and uncle had been with him when he'd been young: kindly but a bit bemused. It was, perhaps, how Seph's family was with her. They didn't truly know her, he realised. They'd never either been given or looked for the chance.

Then, he realised in the next moment, his own brand of acid was being poured onto his wound as Seph replied, her tone utterly scathing.

"As if I'd dress to impress for a wet schoolboy like that," she scoffed, a sneering edge to her voice that lacerated Oliver's ego in a single sweeping slice. "He's like a puppy begging to be kicked." For good measure she made a puppy-like face, panting, tongue out, utterly cringeworthy. "Pathetic," she finished, a ringing pronouncement, and Oliver didn't wait for anything more.

He turned quickly on his heel, blind to everyone around him, no doubt crimson to the tips of his ears, and Seph's awful words ringing in them. *Wet schoolboy. Puppy. Pathetic.* Shame, hurt, and rage all jostled for space in his wounded soul as he rushed out of the hall as fast as he could, mindless of where he was going, wanting only to escape.

When he reached the kitchen, he realised he was still carrying the stupid platter of canapés; he dumped them on the table, shrugged out of the absurd smoking jacket, and then strode out into the night.

Chapter Eight

"U H-OH."

Sam had the grace to look guilty as Oliver stormed past them and Seph whirled towards her brother. "Did you know he was there?" she cried, and he shrugged.

"I've been at the hospital with Rose, so I haven't actually met him properly yet, but he was wearing Dad's smoking jacket and he looked sort of like Harry Potter. Is that Oliver?"

"Oh!" Seph cried, furious and yet also near tears. *Why* had Sam teased her? And why had she risen so willingly to the bait, and said such awful, cruel things?

"You can apologise, Seph," Sam offered. "A genuine sorry goes a long way, trust me."

Not that far, Seph thought, filled with a deep, plunging despondency that felt like grief. How could she have said all that? The insults had spilled from her lips in a panic born of Sam's good-natured teasing; she should have shrugged it all off, but she'd already felt so prickly and vulnerable, in this stupid dress, with her stupid hair.

Everything was stupid, especially her.

"It's not like you care about him or anything," Sam offered reasonably, and Seph glared at him. Her brother was stupid, too. The *stupidest*.

"You don't know what you're talking about," she snapped.

"I don't?" Realisation was dawning on her brother's face, but Seph didn't have the time or patience for it.

"Just keep out of my business," she barked, and then she hurried out of the hall, after Oliver.

She didn't know where he was, and as she hurried down the hall towards the kitchen, she realised she wasn't sure she actually wanted to find him. He'd be furious, and rightly so. Maybe he would be cruel, or worse, dismissive. Or worse than that, he'd be hurt, and she won't know how to deal with that at all.

Seph skidded to a stop outside the kitchen, her breath coming in ragged pants. What should she do? Her first instinct was to find Oliver and explain, but her second one, just as strong, was to protect herself. She already felt vulnerable enough, without her dreadlocks, in this dress. She needed *some* kind of armour for the confrontation they were likely to have.

Besides, she reasoned, Oliver might need some time to—what? Cool down? Recollect his composure? Or maybe he wasn't that bothered. The possibility brought both relief and alarm. Maybe he'd laugh at her and tell her *he'd* been feeling sorry for her—of course he had—and really, wasn't she the one who was puppyish and pathetic?

The more Seph considered the matter, the more she thought it was likely he'd scoff. Of course he would, and he'd be right to. Slowly she retraced her steps away from the kitchen, skirted the hall, and went out the side to the stables and the safety of her workshop.

As soon as she stepped into the cool, dim space she felt a rush of relief. She was safe here. She knew who she was with a lathe or a chisel; she didn't have to pretend to be anyone else. She didn't have to try to be tough or uncaring or bored; she could just *be*, with no one looking, staring, whispering, wondering. She took a deep breath and ran a hand through her hair, shocked all over again by how short it was. How different she looked. She'd wanted to fit in, and yet right now she felt even more like a freak.

She glanced at her sculpture, hidden under a drop cloth, and then with a sudden, heady feeling of recklessness, she drew the drop cloth off. The hunk of wood was just as she'd left it—half rugged, wild and unformed, half polished and perfect, a tangled mess of surprising symmetry...which was exactly how she felt. *Out of the Wild*, she'd called it, because that was how she'd felt too—as if she were emerging from a jungle, or perhaps a chrysalis, fighting her way out even as she kept shrinking back, never knowing what to do or how to do it.

Tonight she'd taken a few tottering steps, and now it was

time to scuttle back in. It was safer here, she thought, hiding away. Pretending not to care. Why had she ever thought she could do something—anything—differently?

She stayed in her shop, working on a new piece, until nearly eleven, when she figured everyone else would have gone to bed and it would be safe to creep up to her own bedroom, unnoticed. She turned out the lights and locked up, pausing for a moment to gaze at the garden, its frost-tipped trees and shrubs sparkling under a sliver of moon. The air was cold and clear, and she relished the solitude, the silence broken by the mournful hoot of a barn owl.

Then she walked inside.

"Seph, where have you *been*?"

So not everyone had gone to bed. Olivia and Althea were sat at the table with the last of the sherry between them, their heels kicked off.

"We were looking for you," Olivia said. "I wanted to show you off to everyone."

Show her off? Seph shook her head as she went to the sink to wash the wood dust from her hands. "I needed to work."

"On a Friday evening? When we had an occasion?" Althea sounded somewhere between sceptical and condemning.

"I'm not exactly an asset at these functions," Seph replied shortly. "And I don't enjoy them."

"I thought you might be with Oliver," Olivia chimed in, a teasing note in her voice. "He disappeared around the same time you did."

"Oh?" Althea's voice sharpened with interest. "Well, well, well."

"Don't," Seph said, too tired to be angry. "It's not like that."

"But it could be—" Olivia began, and Seph stopped her with a shake of her head.

"Don't."

Olivia peered closely at her. "Seph, are you okay?" she asked gently.

Seph bit her lip. She felt, in that moment, perilously close to tears, and she really didn't want to cry, not when she needed to be tough.

She took a deep breath to steady herself. "I'm fine," she said firmly.

"Did something happen? Sam mentioned he'd said something—"

"Forget it." Now she sounded like her usual sulky self. "Just...stop with the speculation, okay? I don't need it, and frankly you managed fine not thinking about me at all for most of my life." She spoke matter-of-factly, but Olivia and Althea both blinked, looking hurt and guilty.

"We're here now, Seph—" Althea began, and Olivia interjected, "And we do care about you, you know."

"I know." Her throat was growing tight. She could not have this conversation now, not on top of everything else that had happened this evening. "It's late. I need to go to bed."

Olivia and Althea both looked like they wanted to say a lot more, but amazingly, they kept themselves from it.

"Well, you know you can talk to us, if you need to?" Olivia said and Seph nodded mechanically. She knew Olivia meant it and sure, she could talk to them, these sisters of hers who had never been around, not when she'd got her first period, or been bullied at school, or felt so lonely and weird she could drown in the emotions.

They'd dipped in and out of her life with careless ease— at one point, Seph had gone three years without seeing Althea, who had looked mildly surprised to clap eyes on her when she'd come back to the castle. Seph suspected her sister had genuinely forgotten she existed. Not one of them had ever really acknowledged that it might be a little tough, growing up with elderly, eccentric parents who'd had their heyday of childrearing twenty years earlier. They'd assumed, just like her parents had, that she was happy doing her own thing, that she was satisfyingly self-sufficient.

Well, she'd learned to be, and she certainly wasn't going to talk about what was going on now to either Olivia or Althea.

"Sure, I know," she said, and then she walked out of the room.

As she headed upstairs, she paused by the narrow stairway that led to the servants' quarters where Oliver was sleeping. Of course, she had no intention of going up there now, when he was likely in bed or already asleep. But she lingered for a few seconds, wondering what she'd say when she saw him again, what he would say. Would he brush it off? Ignore her? Act like it hadn't happened at all? Should she apologise—or not even try, because it would probably fall flat or be rejected outright?

She had no idea, because she was hopeless with social situations, as she'd proved tonight. Why should she try at all, with anyone? What was the point, when it led to more uncertainty, unhappiness, this restless feeling inside her worse than ever? With a dispirited sigh, Seph turned from the stairs and headed to her room.

❄

OLIVER WAS DOING his best not to feel stung. No, not stung, he acknowledged as he dressed for the day, intending to head up to the orchard before anyone else was up. *Hurt.* He was actually really hurt, which felt, well, as pathetic as Seph had said he was. *Like a puppy begging to be kicked.* It was so close to what Jack used to sneer at him that Oliver still cringed when he thought about those words coming out of her mouth.

Had she meant them? Did it matter? She'd said them, to her brother no less, and that was bad enough. And yes, Oliver had always known he had a tendency to people-please, born of, no doubt, the insecurity of being rejected by his own mother. The trouble was, knowing your own weaknesses didn't make hearing someone else sneer about them any easier. In fact, it rather made it worse.

Well, now he knew, Oliver told himself as he filled a flask with coffee, made a quick bacon sandwich, and headed outside, determined to see absolutely no one. He'd left the party last night like a schoolgirl in a strop, which was bad enough, especially considering he'd been meant to serve canapés all evening.

He'd walked through the walled garden instead, and then hiked up to the campsite, shut down now for winter. He'd wandered through the wood, happy to empty out his mind and lose track of time in the process. By the time he'd made it back to the castle, all the guests had left, and so he'd headed upstairs without seeing anyone, which had been a relief.

And he still wasn't ready to have any awkward conversations with anyone, so he'd spend several hours this morning clearing brambles and working up a sweat and hopefully getting Seph out of his system.

Unfortunately it wasn't that easy. Yes, he worked up a sweat, and he cleared plenty of brambles, under a wintry pale blue sky and air that felt like a drink of cold water. But he didn't get Seph out of his system. Instead of caring less, he found himself caring more. He was actually getting angry, which felt novel, because he usually backtracked, doubling down on his apologies, insisting everything was his fault. Not this time.

He'd reached out to Seph; he'd thought they were becoming friends. The way she'd spoken to Sam, so completely derisively, had scarred his soul. All right, perhaps that was a *slight* exaggeration, but still, it had both surprised and hurt him. A lot. Had he read her completely wrong, seeing vulnerability where there wasn't any? Or had she lashed out like that because she'd been put on the defensive?

In the end he decided it didn't really matter. Either way, she'd acted like a big jerk—and she hadn't even bothered to apologise, and he knew she'd seen him because he'd watched her eyes widen in surprised horror before he'd walked out of the room. Well, fine. Whatever. He'd misjudged her completely; not the first time he'd done such a thing.

He thought of Audrey, at Oxford, whom he'd thought he'd been having a pretty serious relationship with. They'd dated for two years, which had felt like a long time to Oliver, but when, right before graduation, he'd mentioned future steps—nothing too crazy, but he'd semi-assumed he'd been on fairly firm ground, she'd looked horrified.

"Ollie…" (she was the only one who called him that; he didn't actually like it) "I don't think… I mean, this has been fun, but…we were never serious, you know?"

He'd stared at her, feeling both gormless and at sea. Obviously, he hadn't known. He'd assumed that dating someone for two years, spending most weekends together, meant that the relationship was going somewhere.

"I mean, we can still be friends," she'd said, as if this was somehow going to placate him. "I really do like you…as a friend."

And even though he'd felt like raging at her, he'd gulped and nodded and assured her that yes, of course they could be friends. He liked her as a friend too, and really, considering how different their lives were—she was moving to London and he was hoping to head back to Pembury—well, it all made a lot of sense. By the end of their conversation, he was practically applauding her sensible decision. What a *chump*. What a pathetic, puppyish wet schoolboy he'd been, just as Seph had said.

Well, not this time. Not, he acknowledged, that he and Seph had been anything but acquaintances-almost-friends, but still. He wasn't going to fall all over himself explaining away someone else's cruelty. He was going to stand up for himself for once, if he ever got the chance.

"Oliver?"

He glanced up, wiping the sweat from his brow with his forearm, surprised to see Seph standing at the edge of the orchard, as if he'd conjured her up by sheer force of will. She was back to wearing her usual get-up of dungarees with a plaid shirt and work boots, but her hair was still a short tangle of blonde curls, and it made her look shorn somehow, both gamine and vulnerable. Oliver did his best to harden his far-too-soft heart. Her scathing words from last night were still ringing in his ears, and he was not going to roll over for her or anyone.

"Hey," he said, making sure to keep his tone neutral.

"Althea said you'd be up here."

"And so I am." She blinked at his rather brusque tone, and Oliver was glad. He was done bending over backwards for Seph or anyone, actually. It had never got him very far, after all, and he had more important things to focus on, like Pembury Farm.

She hesitated, brushing the curls from her face, looking so fragile that, in an instant, Oliver almost unbent. *No*, he told himself. *Stay strong. Stay tough, as tough as Seph can be.*

"I, um, just wanted to say...sorry," she offered hesitantly. "For last night."

"What about last night, exactly?" The question, said in such a hard voice, surprised them both. This was the point at which he usually melted like butter, and started tripping over himself to accept an apology, or better yet, apologise himself, whether he needed to or not. He was glad he wasn't now. It felt both strange and strong.

And yet...was his anger an overreaction?

Really, they barely knew each other. A couple of careless comments—he should be able to brush it all off, and yet...he couldn't. And, he knew, he wasn't willing to let her off that easily. Not for his own sake, and maybe not even hers. A free pass never really helped anyone, did it?

Seph blinked at him. "For what I said," she replied after a moment, her tone still hesitant. "To my brother Sam..."

"Oh, right." Oliver slapped his forehead in a parody of remembering. "You mean that thing about me being—let me recall—a wet schoolboy? Or the bit about me being like a puppy begging to be kicked?" He raised his eyebrows, knowing he was digging a hole for himself but too wound up to care. "Or maybe it was that final, ringing pronouncement—*pathetic*. Says it all, really, doesn't it?" Yes, he'd clearly remembered it all, and now she knew it. So what?

Seph looked stricken, her eyes wide as she nibbled her lip. "I didn't mean it," she whispered. "I didn't mean any of it."

"I don't care," Oliver replied recklessly, heady with the novelty of speaking his mind. "Because you know what? It doesn't even matter. Yes, it's true I made an effort with you, because I thought I liked you, and stupid me, I also thought I saw something vulnerable beneath your I-don't-give-a-damn attitude. But I guess I was wrong, and that's all there is." He turned back to the bramble he'd been cutting through, swinging the scythe in a satisfyingly sweeping arc, watching the thorns fall to the ground. "Lesson learned, so thanks for that. I won't bother next time."

He expected her to go then, because he knew he was being something of an arse—even if it felt kind of good—and she wasn't one to take any stick. But she didn't. She simply stood there, staring at him, until, mired in guilt for the way he was acting, he snarled, "What?"

"I...I didn't think you'd be so hurt," she said, sounding both regretful and wondering.

"I'm—" *Not hurt*, was what he was about to say, but

then he thought, *Screw it.* He couldn't pretend not to care and care at the same time, and she'd already accused him of wearing his heart on his sleeve. "Well, I was," he told her shortly. "As I imagine you would have been, if you'd heard me saying the kind of stuff you were, about you. But maybe not." Maybe she wouldn't care at all.

She paled, chewing her lip practically to shreds. "I...I would have been," she admitted quietly. "And I really am sorry. I shouldn't have said such... It's just Sam was teasing me... It's not an excuse," she clarified quickly. "I'm not saying that, just that it's a reason. I've...I've never been good with...social stuff. Of any kind. I say the first thing that pops into my head—"

"Oh, great," Oliver interjected sarcastically. "Is that supposed to make me feel better, that *that* was the first thing that popped into your head?"

"Oliver, no." She took a step towards him, one hand flung out in appeal. "I'm not saying it was. I just...I didn't want Sam figuring out how I really felt."

He was *not* thawing. Not yet, anyway. "Which was?" he asked, his tone as forbidding as he could make it.

Seph hesitated. Oliver could tell she was battling with herself, a need for self-preservation warring with a desire to be honest. Or was he projecting his own emotions onto her...again? Because that was certainly how he felt.

"You're the first person who has actually ever tried with me," she stated quietly, her head lowered, blonde curls falling in front of her face. "Look, I know what I'm like, okay? I'm unfriendly, unpleasant, even rude. I *know* that. And yet you still tried." With her gaze still on the ground, she shook her head slowly, as if she couldn't quite believe that he had, and Oliver folded his arms. He wasn't ready to unbend, not until he figured out where she was going with this.

"And?" he asked after a moment.

"And I didn't know what to do with it," she confessed, giving him a quick glance upwards before she hid behind her hair again. "I still don't. How to respond. I just…didn't have the…" she shrugged "…the experience or the skills or anything. And so I acted like a big jerk, because I felt so…exposed. I really am sorry. I have this awful tendency to do that because I don't know how else to be. I really wish I hadn't with you."

"Technically, it was with Sam."

She gave him the ghost of a smile then, which almost had him smiling back. He was discovering it was far more pleasant to be easy-going rather than angry, and yet, even so he couldn't quite let go of his hurt.

"Either way," she said, facing him head-on for the first time. "I'm sorry. Truly. Can we please…start again?"

Oliver hesitated, his gaze moving upwards to the bright blue sky as he scratched his cheek. What did start again even mean? They'd barely started, after all. They'd had one sort-of date, not even that. It occurred to him then that his reactions to Seph had all been out of whack—from his determination to get to know her, to win her over, to the hurt he'd felt at her throwaway comments last night.

He needed to calm the hell down, he decided. Start acting like a sensible grown-up rather than some...drama queen. And he definitely needed to stop *caring* so much. Jeez. When was he going to grow up and stop being such a damned people-pleaser?

"Sure," he said, and he stuck the scythe in the ground as he gave what he hoped was a careless shrug. "We can start over. Why not?"

That didn't seem to be quite the answer Seph was looking for, because her expression clouded as she slowly nodded. "Okay," she said slowly. "Great. I'm glad. Thank you."

Oliver nodded back and picked up his scythe. After a few moments where the only sound was the sweep of it through the brambles, Seph forlornly picked her way out of the orchard and headed back down to the castle.

Chapter Nine

SEPH WAS LOST in thought all the way back to the castle. Her boots clumped through the frost-tipped ground as she traced her steps back through the wood, down the hill, and then through the walled garden, her mind spinning and sifting through all she'd learned in that short, painful conversation with Oliver.

He was willing to start their friendship over. That was a good thing, even if the way he'd said it had hurt, like he didn't really care either way. But he *had* to care, at least a little, Seph thought, to have been so hurt. Right?

She'd been so surprised by that. Surprised and gratified and alarmed all at once, that she'd affected him so much. For most of her life she'd felt as if she hadn't affected anyone at all, because no one actually cared enough. All right, that was perhaps being a bit too self-pitying. She knew her parents loved her, even if they seemed to forget about her half the time. She didn't actually doubt that, and yet she didn't always *feel* it, either, but maybe that was her own fault, at least in part. She had chosen to act rather unlovable, indifferent to the people she was supposed to care about most.

Not a great way to be, really—for her or her family.

Seph stopped right there in the garden as the realisation washed over her. She'd made a rod for her own back, by being so prickly, difficult, and defensive. A rod for her own back and her own worst enemy—pushing people away when what she really wanted was to be loved and accepted. Making it hard for them to love her, even if they wanted to.

She thought about Olivia and Althea last night, telling her she could talk to them, that they cared. What if it hadn't been the kind of throwaway remark she had always assumed them to be making? What if they'd been trying, and she'd basically turned her back, because it felt easier? Or at least safer.

Slowly she sat down on a wrought-iron bench against the garden wall, staring blankly into space, mindless of the icy iron beneath her. She'd always been of the don't-let-them-hurt-you-first mentality, but she'd known for a while now that that hadn't got her very far. She'd still been hurt by the seeming indifference, and she'd made it impossible to show it. Talk about shooting yourself in the foot...or really, the heart.

But could she be different now? Different with Oliver, and different with everyone else, to boot? She thought of Sam's words last night: *Who are you trying to impress?* He'd only been teasing—she'd *known* that—and yet it had still felt excruciating because she didn't want to try and fail. She didn't want to offer up even a little piece of her heart and have it rejected.

But maybe the alternative, of keeping the whole thing to herself, was worse. Far worse.

But what would trying even look like? With Oliver? With her family?

"Seph, there you are!"

Seph looked up, blinking in surprise to see Olivia bustling towards her. "The seamstress has arrived with all our dresses! You're going to try yours on, aren't you?"

"Dresses?" she repeated blankly.

Olivia shook her head, smiling. "What are you like? Don't you remember, for Althea's wedding? The wedding that is in less than a month?"

"I'm wearing a dress? Again?"

"Why do you think I gave you a dress rehearsal last night?" Olivia returned with a laugh. "I'm trying to ease you in gently. Because you have to wear your bridesmaid dress, Seph, and heels. Sorry."

"Wait," Seph said, blinking up at her sister. "I'm a bridesmaid?"

Olivia shook her head. "Althea asked us both a few months ago. Don't you remember?"

Had Althea said something about it? Seph recalled Althea talking about bridesmaids, and she'd assumed she'd have Olivia, like she did for her wedding to Jasper when Seph had only been two. She'd excluded herself automatically, and maybe she shouldn't have.

"I didn't realise…" she began, only to have Olivia pull her up by the hand.

"Well, you do now! Come and try on your dress."

"All right…"

"Rose and Sam are bringing the twins back tomorrow afternoon, you know," Olivia continued as she hurried Seph along the garden paths. "You definitely don't want to miss that!"

"I suppose not." She'd kept a very low profile with all the family doings; yes, she'd known Althea and John were getting married and yes, she was well aware Rose and Sam had had twins, but she hadn't really thought beyond that. She hadn't inserted herself into any of the family gatherings or plannings, because…well, she never had before. But maybe this was what trying could look like.

"Hurry up," Olivia called to her, for Seph's steps had slowed on the path. "The seamstress Tilly is waiting to take our measurements for alterations. What were you doing out here, anyway? It's freezing."

"Just thinking—"

"They must have been some very deep thoughts." Olivia paused to peer at her closely. "Is everything okay? I know I asked you last night, but I'll ask again because Sam said something about maybe having upset you—"

"He didn't," Seph said quickly. Her brother hadn't meant anything by his teasing; she knew that. She was the one who had created the conflict. She just hoped Oliver could move past it like he'd said. "Anyway, let's go see these dresses."

"They're gorgeous. And not too frilly, or anything like that, so I think you'll like them, too." Sliding her a quick, sideways grin, Olivia hurried back towards the castle, with Seph following.

Althea had turned the family sitting room above the kitchen into something of a dressing room, with plastic-swathed hangers everywhere and Tilly, the local seamstress, equipped with a tape measure and pincushion. Someone had even dragged a lacquered coromandel screen that one of their ancestors had picked up during their travels to Asia from the attic, for modesty while changing.

"I'm not sure I need a new dress," Violet mused as the seamstress began taking the plastic off the dresses. "I've got so many things in my closet…"

"And most of them are at least forty years old if not one hundred and forty years old," Althea replied briskly. "They're lovely vintage, Mummy, but I think you deserve a new dress, and royal blue is such a lovely colour on you. Brings out your eyes."

Violet smiled faintly as she touched her hair, drawn up in a messy bun with a knitting needle stuck through it. "My eyes are one of my best features," she agreed, and Olivia gave Seph a laughing look.

"If you do so say yourself, Mum," she teased. "But you

first, Althea. Let's see your gorgeous gown!"

"It's more sensible than gorgeous," Althea replied, "which is perfectly appropriate for a bride in her forties, on a second marriage no less—"

"Oh, come on." Olivia rolled her eyes. "Don't take away *all* the romance."

Althea's cheeks pinked. "There's still plenty of romance, I assure you," she said stiffly, and Olivia let out a howl of laughter while Seph found herself smiling. It wasn't often her oldest sister looked discomfited.

"Bridesmaids first, anyway," Althea said briskly. "Olivia and Seph, come on now."

"How did I manage to forget I was a bridesmaid?" Seph asked, and then blushed at Althea's knowing look.

"Maybe because you weren't thrilled at the thought of wearing a dress," she replied. "Which is why I was so pleased to see you in one last night, because clearly you can dress up when the mood strikes you."

"Yes, but…" Seph wasn't sure how to explain that she'd never *expected* to be a bridesmaid. That she and Althea had never had that kind of relationship.

"I want both my sisters to be bridesmaids," Althea declared robustly.

"What about Poppy?" Seph asked. Althea's eighteen-year-old daughter had just started university.

"She's doing a reading during the ceremony. We wanted to keep it streamlined and simple. Two sisters, two bridesmaids." She paused and then continued with an awkward sort of determination, "I know we haven't always been as close as we could have been, but I am trying to make up for that. Probably not doing a very good job of it, but still." She gave Seph a suspiciously bright-eyed smile. "Here we all are."

"Yes." Seph found she was as alarmingly bright-eyed as Althea. "Here we are."

Her sister was clearly making an effort to include her, and so, she decided, she would make an effort too. She would try, even if everyone knew she was trying, even if it was hard.

"That's okay, isn't it, Seph?" Althea asked, an uncharacteristic note of uncertainty in her voice. "I know you don't like dressing up, but the dresses are really quite elegant and simple—"

"It's fine," Seph said quickly. She took a steadying breath and then continued, "I mean, it's more than fine. It's great. Thank you. I'm honoured. And touched, actually. I never expected you to ask me, so…thank you. Really." The resounding silence that followed this made Seph blush and prickle, just a little bit. "What?" she asked. Okay, so maybe she'd tried a little too much.

"Nothing," Althea said after a moment. "I'm just…really glad you feel that way."

All right, that wasn't so bad. Seph gave a twitchy little shrug. "Good."

Althea glanced at Olivia, and Seph felt herself start to

prickle again. "What?" she asked, her voice sharpening a little.

"I think Althea is just a bit surprised at how accommodating you're being, darling," Violet chimed in. "You can get your back up, can't you? Just like your aunt Matilda."

This only made Seph prickle all the more and for a second one of her usual retorts rose like a bubble in her throat but then she made herself swallow it down. "I didn't even know we had an aunt Matilda," she managed.

"Well, technically she was a cousin. Or maybe a second cousin. On your father's side. She came to our wedding... She was horribly offended that we didn't ask her to do a reading, but the truth was I'd never even met her before. That was the last we saw of her, I think...and also the last we saw of a pair of Meissen shepherdesses."

Althea let out a choking laugh. "Are you saying she stole them?"

Violet shrugged, unperturbed. "They were her wedding present, to be fair. I suppose she decided to take them back."

And this was the person she was like? Seph glanced at Althea and Olivia, who gave her commiserating smiles that suddenly had her smiling back, as if they were all sharing a joke while their mother continued to reflect on the moody Aunt Matilda.

"So let's see this dress," Seph finally said.

"Of course." Tilly had finished unwrapping the plastic from the hangers and she handed the first dress to Althea, who held it up. "This is yours," she said to Seph as she handed her a hanger. "Olivia's is a bit more flowing, but they're both in the same fabric. Do you want to try it on?" She nodded towards the screen.

"Okay." Seph stroked the soft velvet as she took the dress behind the screen. It was a simple sheath in forest green, with a darker green satin band around the empire waist, and cap sleeves.

"Very Jane Austen," Olivia remarked as she took her own dress. "While mine is a bit more Goth fairy tale."

"I thought they'd suit your personalities," Althea replied. "Simple for Seph, and a bit more frou-frou for you."

"I'll take that as a compliment," Olivia replied with a laugh, "as I am sure Seph will."

"I'm definitely not frou-frou," Seph replied with a shudder. She wasn't even sure what that meant, but she thought she could guess.

"Try it on then," Althea urged, and quickly Seph scrambled out of her clothes and then slipped on the dress. It fit snugly, skimming her breasts and hips, before falling straight all the way to her ankles. She smoothed her hands over the soft material, once more amazed at the transformation a simple dress could cause. Even more than last night, when she'd worn Olivia's dress, this outfit made her look like a different person. Feel like a different person. Like someone she might one day want to be. And really, she was already taking tiny steps towards becoming that person, simply by being here.

"Well?" Althea asked, and slowly, shyly, Seph ventured out from behind the screen.

"Oh, Seph!" Olivia exclaimed, and Violet turned misty-eyed.

"Oh, darling," she said. "You look beautiful. Just as I did at your age. We have the same colouring, you know—"

"We all have the same colouring, Mum," Althea reminded her.

"Short hair really suits you," Olivia said frankly. "So curly! I always wanted curly hair. Where did that gene come from, I wonder?"

"Your great-aunt Winifred, on your father's side," Violet replied immediately. "She had absolute ringlets, right into old age. Very proud of them, too. Insisted she'd never had a perm, but I did wonder sometimes." She gave Seph an affectionate smile. "Really, darling, you look so lovely. I don't know why you hide that figure of yours! If I had a waist that small, I'd be cinching it with a belt every day of my life."

"Surely you had a waist that small when you were younger," Althea teased, and Violet considered the matter seriously.

"Not quite as small," she allowed after a moment, "but almost."

"What do you think, Seph?" Althea asked, her tone turning serious. "Can you stomach wearing it for a day? I know you'd rather be in dungarees and boots—"

"No, it's fine," Seph said quickly. "I mean, it's…better than fine." She smiled hesitantly. "I think I actually sort of like it."

Again, this was met with a thunderclap of silence. She saw Olivia and Althea exchange glances. "What?" she demanded. She was trying not to go all prickly, but it was hard.

"Nothing, nothing," Olivia said quickly. "It's wonderful that you like it. And you look gorgeous. Now I'll try on mine."

Olivia looked just as gorgeous in her more 'frou-frou' dress, with its flowing skirt and long sleeves. She twirled extravagantly before Tilly got busy with both of them, measuring and pinning, and then Violet tried on her dress, a simple sheath in royal-blue crepe.

"Perhaps a bit of embellishment?" she suggested hopefully to Tilly. "A bit of lace, or if that's too young, then some nice beadwork along the neckline?" She glanced at Althea. "Really, darling, I thought you knew me better. I never wear anything plain."

"I tried," Althea mouthed to both Olivia and Seph, and once again Seph found herself smiling, struggling to hold in an unexpected laugh.

"Now your turn," Olivia cried, and grinning, Althea ducked behind the screen. When she came out again, everyone oohed and aahed at the sight of her in a simple column dress of cream satin, with a matching bolero jacket trimmed in cream velvet.

"You look like the ice queen," Olivia exclaimed. "But nicer, of course. Much nicer. Not icy at all, really."

"Well, I didn't feel I could go too crazy, considering," Althea said as she studied her reflection. "You don't think I look too mutton-dressed-as-lamb?"

"Not at all!" Olivia assured her. "You look thirty-five at the absolute oldest."

"Well, here's hoping." Althea let out a shaky laugh as she ran a hand down the length of her dress. Seph was surprised to see how nervous and uncertain her sister seemed. Althea always seemed so confident, annoyingly so, yet right there, as she gazed at herself in the mirror, she looked vulnerable.

Maybe *everyone* was vulnerable, in one way or another, Seph reflected. Some people just hid it better. She thought of Oliver again, seeming so hurt, and along with a pang of remorse she felt a flicker of hope. They *would* start over, she thought fiercely. *She* would. She already was.

"I think this calls for champagne," Violet announced after Tilly had taken the dresses away to be altered. "All my gorgeous girls together! There's a bottle of Dom Pérignon in the cellar. I'm going to bring it out."

"Oh, Mummy, you don't have to—" Althea protested, and Violet spread her arms out extravagantly.

"Why shouldn't we celebrate? It's not often we're all together like this, sharing each other's company." Her gaze, turning shrewd as it so often could, rested on each of them. "I want to celebrate all of you. And what better way to do that than with oodles of champagne?"

"I think that Dom Perignon is worth a thousand pounds or something," Althea whispered as Violet went downstairs. "And I have a feeling Daddy was saving it for something special."

"Well, maybe this is something special," Olivia replied. "You're getting married, the castle has been a success, and we're all together." She lifted her shoulders in a smiling shrug. "Why shouldn't we celebrate?"

Althea looked as if she was going to protest but then she laughed and shrugged back. "You're right. Why not? *Carpe diem*, and all that. Right, Seph?" She glanced at Seph, smiling, and Seph smiled back.

"Right."

Carpe diem. Truer words, she thought, had never been spoken.

Violet returned a few moments later, brandishing a dusty bottle in one hand, and some vintage coupe glasses in the other.

"Who wants to do the honours?" she asked, and Seph found herself saying, "I will."

If anyone was surprised by her willingness to engage, they didn't show it, and Seph took the bottle, popping the cork with deft aplomb while everyone clapped. She was smiling again, she realised, more than she had in a long time.

It felt good, even though her cheeks, unused to the effort, ached.

She poured champagne into all the glasses and then they raised them in a toast as Violet declared grandly, "To us!"

"To us," they chorused back, and then everyone took a sip of the cold, crisp champagne.

"I feel positively decadent," Olivia remarked. "Sipping champagne at eleven o'clock in the morning!"

"Your aunt Matilda always started the day with a mimosa," Violet remarked. "Without fail."

"Is this the same Aunt Matilda who was a moody kleptomaniac?" Althea asked. "Why have we never heard of her before?"

"No, it was a different one," Violet replied seriously. "An actual aunt, rather than a cousin. She died when you were quite young. She was your great-aunt, actually, I suppose. She used to come to Casterglass for a month every summer. She played a marvellous game of bridge."

Olivia raised her eyebrows. "We had *two* Aunt Matildas?"

"Yes, I suppose you did," Violet mused with a tone of surprise. "I suppose it was a more common name, back in the day. Strange, though...I've never been partial to it, myself. As a name, I mean. Although your aunt Matilda was lovely. Not the one who took the shepherdesses, of course..." She shook her head as she took another sip of champagne. Olivia met Seph and Althea's glances and suddenly, as if they'd rehearsed it, all three of them burst out laughing.

Seph couldn't remember the last time she'd laughed like this, if she ever had, so her stomach hurt and her cheeks stretched and she felt as if she were floating inside. It felt *good* to laugh. It felt healing, like she was letting go the parts of herself she'd held on to for far too long. The hurt, the bitterness, the resentment, the insecurity. Oh, they were all still there—she knew that. Shedding such old habits and hurts wasn't so easy that they slipped away with no more than a belly laugh and a glass of champagne. But she'd loosened her hold on them, just a little bit, and for that Seph was grateful.

Change was possible. Fresh starts did happen. And today, she thought as she swallowed the last of her champagne, was a brand-new day.

Chapter Ten

S EPH WAS JUST finishing up in her workshop when there
was a quick, light knock at the door.

"Yes?" she called, switching off the lathe and lowering
her safety goggles.

Oliver poked his head around the door and her heart did
a funny little leap. They hadn't spoken alone together since
the orchard yesterday, but things had felt a bit easier all the
same. He'd smiled at her at supper last night, and afterwards
he'd dried the dishes while Olivia washed up and she'd
wiped the table and, all in all, it had felt fairly companionable, even if they hadn't said much.

But what did he want now?

"Hi," he said, and Seph realised she was staring.

"Hi."

"May I come in?"

The question, asked so politely, reminded her of how
she'd freaked out just a few days before, and she cringed
inwardly.

"Yes, of course you can." She wiped her dusty hands on

her work apron as Oliver stepped into her workshop. "How…how are you?"

"Good. How are you?"

"Good."

He nodded and they both stood there silently for a moment before Oliver shot her a wry grin. "Wow, we really are starting over, aren't we?"

A burst of nervous laughter escaped her like gunfire as Seph nodded, a bit frantically. "Yes, I suppose we are."

He glanced around the workshop, his obvious curiosity making Seph want to both preen and squirm. "This is so cool," he said. "How did you get into woodworking in the first place?"

"John Braithwaite showed me."

"Althea's fiancé?"

"Yes, I used to help out on his farm, when I was younger. He did some woodworking himself, and when I was about fifteen or so he showed me how. I was hooked."

"That was kind of him."

"Yes, it really was." John had been tirelessly kind, Seph reflected, even if she hadn't always acknowledged it. He'd given her jobs when she'd needed something to do, and a mug of strong, sweet tea and a slab of cake when he must have sensed that she'd felt lonely or out of sorts. They'd never talked about feelings—Seph didn't think she could have stood it if John had tried—but he'd always been there, even when he'd been going through his own trials, with his wife having left him and then returning only when she had terminal cancer and needed care. John had nursed her until she had died, and Seph had stopped coming around for a while, because she hadn't wanted to be a burden, but when it had all been over, John had welcomed her back and she'd felt guilty, for staying away. Maybe he could have used a friend. Maybe everyone could.

"So," Oliver said, bringing her thoughts back to the present, "I need your help."

"You do?"

"Althea said you know this place better than anyone."

"I suppose so," Seph replied after a moment. "Except for my parents, perhaps. My father was born here, after all."

"Yes, but they seem a bit...distracted sometimes." Oliver gave her another one of those wry smiles that made her heart stupidly flutter.

"Too true," she agreed.

"And Althea thought your knowledge would be a tiny bit more up to date," he continued, "so...I wanted to ask, do you know where you might find a cider press?"

"A cider press?" Seph raised her eyebrows. "Does this have something to do with the orchard?"

"Well, hypothetically, I suppose. Althea's quite keen to make the orchard a going concern, and so I was hoping that part of the attraction could be cider making." He shrugged, spreading his hands. "All these artisanal type classes seem to be taking off...cider making, sourdough bread starting, foraging for hedge trimmings…"

Seph let out a laugh. "That's your salad sorted, then," she said, and Oliver somehow managed to grin and grimace at the same time, making her laugh again. Were they having proper banter, she wondered, or even *flirting*? It felt miraculous—and also a little bit alarming. "A cider press," she repeated, turning away in case she was blushing too hard. "I'm not sure, but I think I might know where one is. At least, where one could be. We could look, anyway."

"Wonderful," Oliver replied, his tone heartfelt. "Are you free now? Otherwise, I can come back…?"

"I'm free now." Seph slipped off her apron and hung it on a peg. As she tucked her curls behind her ears, she wished she'd worn something a bit more flattering—but what? And for woodworking? She was turning into such a ninny. "I was just finishing up yet another planter," she continued, "and frankly I'm getting a bit tired of those, so…"

"Do you sell your own sculptures?" Oliver asked. "I mean, artistic pieces, and not just planters and things?"

Seph tensed, wondering if he was going to bring up her whole overreaction to him seeing *Out of the Wild*, and then she shook her head. "No, I don't. I don't have many, and in any case, they feel too private." Her tone had started to turn terse, and she tried to moderate it. "For that kind of public viewing, anyway. I just make them for me."

Even though she'd tamed her tone, Oliver winced. "I really was an unforgivable snoop, coming in here the other day. I'm sorry."

"Not *unforgivable*," she replied, and he gave her a quick smile.

"Thank you for that. And thank you for making that sculpture. I know I wasn't supposed to see it, but it really was incredible. I hope you know that."

Now she was definitely blushing. "It was just something I thought of," she half-mumbled. "I don't know that it's very good."

"It's amazing," Oliver stated firmly. "I'm sure you could make a name for yourself, as a proper artist, if you wanted to." Then, perhaps sensing her embarrassment at so many fulsome compliments, he continued, "Now let's see if we can find this cider press."

They stepped out into the empty courtyard, under a crisp blue sky. No one was about, for which Seph was grateful. As hard as she was trying to be different, she didn't think she could have borne one of her siblings' speculative looks just then, not when things were just starting to get on an even keel with Oliver.

"We should look in one of the storage barns," she told him. "They're past the stables here, on the other side of the drive."

"Lead on, MacDuff," Oliver returned grandly, and smiling a little, Seph did.

The storage barns were enormous, made of stone with roofs that had been falling in, but which Althea had had repaired in the last year—yet another one of the important projects she'd quietly arranged, without much fuss. They stored all manner of things—broken-down garden equipment, furniture from the castle that no longer had a place, piles of bricks or roof tiles, stacks of rotting lumber, and various ancient antiques, both junk and treasures. The last time Seph had been in there she'd spied an Edwardian croquet set and a set of child's toy hoops from the Victorian age.

"We should have brought a torch," she remarked as she opened one of the large doors with a rusty-sounding creak. Inside furniture was stacked every which way, piled almost all the way to the ceiling high above, lost in the gloom.

"I have a torch on my phone if it gets too dark," Oliver said as he stepped into the musty darkness to stand next to her. "Goodness. This looks like the Room of Requirement in *Harry Potter*." This made Seph smile, and he glanced at her, a rather knowing gleam in his eye. "What?"

"Only that you look a bit like Harry Potter. Grown up, I mean."

"I have been told that before," he admitted, and she added quickly, "It's meant to be a compliment."

"Is it? Well, I'll take it, then. Now." He looked around, his hands planted on his hips. "Where do we start?"

"Good question." He was standing close enough so his shoulder was almost brushing hers, and she could smell the woodsy scent of his aftershave. It tickled her nostrils, making her want to sneeze. Or maybe that was all the dust. In any case, she felt all strangely tingly inside.

"I guess just go bit by bit?" Oliver suggested as he peered into the barn. "Is that a rocking horse?"

"There's a lot of strange stuff in here," Seph told him. "And up in the attic, as well. My parents never threw anything anyway."

"Neither did their ancestors, it seems, judging by some of this stuff. This looks Georgian." He pointed to a chamber pot perched precariously on top of a chair. "It could go to a museum. Or be sold for a goodly sum."

"My father has sold bits and pieces, to finance this place," Seph replied. "Although a lot of these things are knock-offs, apparently, and not worth much. One of my great-grandfathers, I can't remember which, was something of a collector—of junk."

Oliver shook his head slowly. "I can't imagine having so much history."

Seph stepped into the darkness, running her hand along an elaborately carved table leg from the Victorian period, like nothing you'd see today. She could not imagine carving such a thing, yet she admired the obvious expertise. "There must be a lot of history at Pembury Farm?" she ventured.

"Not like this. Not anywhere close. And in any case, it's not really mine."

"But you're related to the family? The earl?"

Oliver grimaced. "I wish I'd never mentioned that earl.

The title died out over a hundred years ago. Stupid, really, but like you, I have a tendency to say whatever pops into my head." He gave her a smile that managed to be both shy and knowing, and Seph wasn't sure how to respond to this gentle sort of teasing. Her instinct was still to prickle, and yet...she wasn't. She was smiling.

"The things that pop into your head seem a lot nicer than the ones that pop into mine."

"Sometimes," he allowed, "but they can be remarkably stupid. I got called on by a teacher once, for daydreaming, and when she asked me if I knew the answer to her question—I didn't even know what the question *was*—I ended up babbling about how interesting I found her class, and even worse, how much I liked her *skirt*." He shook his head mournfully and Seph stifled a laugh. "She was sixty if she was a day, and I was in year eight. The other kids teased me about having a crush on her for a good year."

"Still," Seph said slowly as they wandered deeper into the shadowy barn, "I think I'd rather be seen as being too kind than too cruel."

"Would you?" Oliver asked, and Seph heard how sceptical he sounded. All right, maybe that wasn't how she'd been acting. In fact, it was the exact opposite of how she'd chosen to live her life—being sullen and rude rather than admitting she cared. Pushing people away rather than daring to let them in.

"I would," she answered honestly, "but I don't think I've

been brave enough to try. It's easier to be cruel than kind, in an awful sort of way."

He stilled, then turned to face her, his expression barely visible in the gloom. "Easier how?"

She shrugged uncomfortably, wondering how they'd ventured into such deep and intimate territory so quickly. "Well, just, you know, if you act as if you don't care so much, then…people can't hurt you."

Feeling like she'd said way too much, she hurried deeper into the barn, peering at a stack of about a dozen chairs all tangled together. "I think it's mainly furniture in here. Maybe we should try the next barn."

"They can still hurt you," Oliver said quietly, making her jump because he'd come up right behind her without her realising. "They just might not know it."

"Well…same difference, I suppose." She was back to mumbling, her gaze fixed on the jumble of chairs, her face burning.

"I don't think it's the same at all. It's worse, because you have to suffer in silence. You can't tell anyone how you really feel."

Which was what she'd realised the other day. Her own worst enemy indeed. "Is that how you are?" she asked, her voice a bit croaky.

Oliver considered the question. "Yes, I suppose it is, but I act like I don't mind because I'm so pleased, rather than because I don't care. My cousin Jack used to tease me for being such a people-pleaser. He'd ask me if I was so afraid that people wouldn't like me, which stung quite a bit, mostly because he was right."

"But I'm sure everyone likes you," Seph protested, genuinely surprised by his admission. "You seem so confident, and friendly, and…I don't know. Nice."

He let out a rather hollow laugh. "Yes, too nice. People seem to sneer at that, for some reason. Call me—well, what you called me. Which was why it hurt." They were both quiet for a moment, and Seph was glad of the dark. She'd been mortified that he'd overheard her the other night, but now she just felt sad. "I'm not bringing that up again to rub your nose in it," Oliver continued quietly. "Just to explain where I'm coming from."

"Thank you," she replied. "And I am sorry—"

"You don't need to say it again."

"I know. But I am. More than I was before, even because I didn't realise. I thought—well I convinced myself you'd brush it off, that you were just being nice because you felt sorry for me."

He took a step closer to her so she could see his face. "Is that what you really thought?"

"I suppose it's what I've always thought. About everyone. Which shows an awful lot of insecurity, I know." She let out a wobbly laugh that trailed off into silence because Oliver was looking at her so intently.

"I don't feel sorry for you, Seph. I admire you. You're

remarkably strong, considering what you've had to deal with in your life."

"It's not like I've had any real tragedy or trial," she protested. Even though she'd acted as if she had. "I've just had a massive chip on my shoulder," she confessed. "Because I felt so lonely." She could hardly believe she was saying these things. It felt wonderfully liberating and completely terrifying at the same time.

"I don't think you do now," Oliver told her. "Or at least you're getting rid of it. Come on." He reached for her hand and Seph let him take it, thrilling to the slide of his palm across hers. "Let's check out the other barn."

He kept hold of her hand all the way to the next barn, but in a way that seemed careless, as if he'd forgotten about it, while Seph felt as if she were holding a stick of dynamite. Was her hand sweaty? Clammy? Hot? Her heart had started beating hard and when Oliver let go to open the door of the barn, she surreptitiously wiped her palm on her dungarees. It had been sweaty, while his had been nice and dry.

"This looks more promising," he called over his shoulder. "I see an old tractor and—I think—a garden gnome."

"That was Olivia," she told him with a laugh. "She bought a whole set from a garden centre that was going out of business, just in case."

"In case of what?" Oliver bent down to inspect the pile of gnomes. "This is magnificent," he said wonderingly. "There's a whole army."

"Just what you need in a crisis."

"Absolutely." He glanced up at her, his teeth flashing in the darkness. "I could spend the rest of my life in these barns and be happy."

So could I, Seph thought, as her heart did another one of those funny little flips. What was happening to her? She turned away, discomfited by the strength of her own feelings. "Let's see if we can find that cider press."

It took half an hour of searching, hefting garden furniture and getting rather dusty, but they finally located an ancient press in the back of the barn, underneath a tattered marquee that had been used for her parents' twenty-fifth anniversary party, decades ago.

"It looks a bit battered," Oliver remarked critically, "but at least it's not rotten. I might be able to get it working."

"Do you know how to operate a cider press?"

"No, but I know how to watch a YouTube video." He grinned at her. "I can become an expert in about four minutes."

She laughed, shaking her head. "See, this is why you seem so confident to me."

"It's all an act, trust me. Can you help me with this?"

Together they hefted the cider press from under the marquee, getting even dustier in the process, and brought it out into the light. It looked even worse for wear in the sunlight, but Oliver's enthusiasm seemed indefatigable.

"There's a spare storeroom in the stables," she told him.

"Next to Ellie's pottery place. You could set it up in there, maybe. I don't think Althea had earmarked it for anything."

"Perfect."

Together they carried it back to the stables, and into the spare storeroom, which needed a good sweeping out but was in otherwise good condition, empty and ready to be used.

"Looks good," Seph said, straightening up, her hands resting on the small of her back.

"It does, doesn't it? Thanks for helping, Seph." He smiled at her, and then, to her shock, he reached forward and brushed her cheeks, his fingers like a whisper against her skin. She opened her mouth, but no sound came out and he smiled wryly as he showed her his dust-streaked fingers. "You had a smear of something on your cheek."

"Oh. Right." Her mouth snapped shut and somehow she managed a smile, even though she felt weak at the knees. What had she thought he'd been doing? She had so little experience with men, with friendship, and most definitely with romance, that the danger of hugely embarrassing herself was alarmingly high. Really, she told herself, she needed to get a grip. She was glad she and Oliver had had a reboot, but they were still very much just friends.

She glanced at him, now inspecting the cider press, his hair ruffled, his shirt straining across his shoulders, and felt her stomach flip. They were just friends...weren't they?

Chapter Eleven

"THIS FEELS LIKE something out of *Downton Abbey*," Oliver muttered to Seph as they stood in a row with everyone else on the driveway, waiting for Sam and Rose to bring their twin daughters, Michaela and Bea, back to Casterglass. It was a grey, drizzly sort of day, and Seph shivered in the autumnal breeze. It was almost December, the darkest part of the year, and although Althea was already getting into festive mode, in preparation for her wedding the week before Christmas, Seph was feeling rather unChristmassy.

Last night she'd learned, while sitting around the kitchen table with everyone after supper, that Althea and John were going on honeymoon for Christmas to somewhere tropical, and bringing Alice, Poppy, Ben and Toby. Olivia and Will were spending Christmas with his parents, who were flying over from Spain to meet her—and of course Will's children Jake and Lally would be going with them—and Rose and Sam were taking the twins to London for the holidays, to meet Rose's mother, which apparently was a big deal because

Rose hadn't seen her mother in years. Then, to top it all off, her parents announced they would be closing the castle for Christmas and going on a cruise.

"You're welcome to come with us, of course, darling," Violet had told her over supper, "but it's for the over-sixties and you're not keen on travel, are you?"

How would her mother know if she was keen on travel, as she'd never done any? It seemed clear that her parents wanted to go on the cruise alone, and so Seph had assured them she'd be fine staying at Casterglass alone—and really, it wasn't such a big deal, she told herself. It wasn't as if they'd had big family Christmases every year. Admittedly, they'd had one last year, when Althea had come home, but before that Christmases had been pretty hit or miss, and mostly miss at that. Sometimes her parents had remembered about things like presents or a tree, but mostly they'd all just done their own things, as usual. Which was what she would do this year, she supposed. She told herself there was no reason to feel out of sorts about it, and yet she did, perhaps because she'd had expectations, without fully acknowledging them to herself, that now that everyone was back at Casterglass, things would be different.

She was trying to be different, but maybe some things would always stay the same.

Seph did her best to push the melancholy thoughts out of her mind as Sam's car came slowly up the drive, and she plastered a welcoming smile onto her face.

"Hell-*o*!"

"Welcome, welcome!"

Everyone clustered around Sam and Rose as they took two car seats out of the car, to a chorus of cooing. Seph stepped closer to take a look at one of the babies, shock jolting through her at the sight of the tiny, wizened creature asleep in her seat.

"Gosh, they're *small*," she said, her tone awed and a little alarmed, and Oliver let out a commiserating whistle.

"Teeny tiny. I have zero experience with infants, I'm afraid. They terrify me slightly, if I'm perfectly honest."

"Me too." Give her a solid hunk of wood any day. Those babies looked as if they could break.

Everyone was heading into the kitchen for celebratory cups of tea, and so Seph and Oliver fell into step behind them. They'd been doing this a lot lately, in the last few days. Gravitating towards each other without actually saying anything or making a big deal of it. Whenever Althea or Olivia started to notice, Seph found herself edging away slightly, hoping Oliver wouldn't notice, not ready for the inevitable speculation and teasing.

She stood to the side in the kitchen as Althea made cups of tea and Rose sat down at the table, a baby in her arms, looking exhausted. Seph had instinctively liked Rose when she'd showed up unexpectedly at the castle in July, pregnant with Sam's child—children, as it turned out—and determined to make a go of it on her own. She was feisty and independent and she'd fallen in love, and that seemed like a good combination to Seph, not that she knew what the third one felt like.

She found herself glancing herself at Oliver, who was studying the babies as if they were scientific specimens, and then she looked away again quickly, before he—or anyone else—noticed.

All right yes, maybe she had a crush. She could be honest enough to admit that. The first kind, cute man who'd walked into her life, and she was smitten. Well, so what? She didn't have to let Oliver know, and she could still enjoy his friendship. Or so she kept telling herself.

"Who wants a cuddle?" Althea asked. She'd been holding one of the babies—Seph could not remotely tell them apart—in a decidedly broody way, although now she was looking beadily around the room, for a waiting pair of empty arms. "Olivia? Will?"

"Oh, ah…" Olivia was blushing, but also gazing at the baby in Althea's arms with an unabashed yearning. Seph fully expected Will to propose soon, perhaps after Althea's wedding, and she supposed he and Olivia would get down to baby making pretty quickly. Her sister was thirty-six, after all, and she desperately wanted a baby.

"Go on, then," Will said affectionately, giving Olivia a little push. "You know you want to."

"Oh, I do." Olivia's arms were practically twitching as she hurried towards Althea and took the baby out of her arms, cuddling her close. "Oh, she's divine," she breathed. "Absolutely divine. And, Rose, you lucky thing, you have two!"

"That's me," Rose replied with a tired smile. "Lucky."

"It must be utterly exhausting," Violet said with some sympathy. "I must confess, when Walter and I were courting, one of the first questions I asked was whether twins ran in the family. I knew a girl at boarding school who ended up marrying a man with twins in the family and they had three sets."

"But twins do run in the family, Mum," Sam said with a laugh. "Hence, these two."

"Yes," Violet agreed rather darkly. "Your father neglected to tell me about his cousins."

"It seemed like such a far-off chance, my dear," Walter replied gallantly, "and I was so determined to marry you."

Olivia was pressing her nose against the baby's downy head. "Why do babies smell so scrumptious?" she asked dreamily. "And why do I feel like I could actually *eat* them?"

"Gerbils sometimes eat their young," Violet mused. "Only the runts, though, apparently to make sure the rest of the litter survives."

"Mum." Olivia let out a horrified laugh. "I didn't mean literally."

"Oh." Violet blinked. "Well, of course not, darling, but I do think it's rather interesting, don't you?"

"Who else wants a cuddle?" Althea asked. "Before Olivia

kidnaps Bea?"

"Actually, that's Michaela," Sam told her. "I think."

"Sam—" Rose sounded horrified.

"I'm kidding, I'm kidding. I know my girls apart." He caught Seph's eye and mouthed, 'Not really.'

Seph choked on a laugh, and it was enough to attract Althea's attention.

"Seph! You haven't had a chance."

"Oh, I don't think—"

"Oh, go on, Seph," Oliver chimed in innocently. "I'm sure you want to. Weren't you telling me how much you wanted a cuddle?"

Seph threw him a disbelieving look before she saw the devilish glint in his eyes. "Oh, but I thought you were telling me the same thing," she returned oh so sweetly. "Weren't you? Good things there are two babies, then."

The look of naked terror on Oliver's face made her choke back another laugh—before Olivia plopped a very tiny baby in her arms.

"Here you go," she said cheerfully.

"Oh but wait." Panicked, Seph cradled the infant close to her chest. She weighed *nothing*. And her head was really rather dangerously floppy. Was that normal?

"Support her head," Rose instructed. "With the palm of your hand."

"But don't poke her in the skull," Violet contributed helpfully. "There's a soft spot, after all. Quite soft, as I discovered when Althea was born."

"I'm not going to *poke* her," Seph cried, appalled, while her family looked on, all of them grinning. They were *enjoying* this.

"And here you go, Oliver," Althea said cheerfully, and his face briefly resembled Munch's *The Scream* as she handed him baby number two.

"Oh, uh, wow. How cute. How…small." Like Seph, he brought the baby to his chest, one large hand under her head, the other spanning her body. "Is this right?" He sounded terrified.

"You're doing it perfectly," Rose assured him. "Naturals, the pair of you."

Which had them glancing at each other and grinning rather foolishly, before they both looked quickly away.

After a few more minutes the babies were whisked away for somebody else's turn, and Seph breathed a silent sigh of relief even as her arms felt weirdly empty. Like Oliver, she had no experience with babies, no reference for them. She'd been ten when Althea's youngest Tobias had been born, but as she'd rarely visited, Althea had hardly seen him, at least until the last year, when he'd been a far more reasonable twelve.

"I'm glad that's over," Oliver said under his breath. "I was afraid I was going to crush her. Which one did I have? Bea or Michaela?"

Seph shrugged helplessly. "I have no idea."

He grinned at her again, and she gave a little laugh. "Guess I'm not very maternal."

"And I'm not paternal, if that's the thing. But we are young, after all."

"Yes, I suppose." Although Seph had never been able to visualise herself with a husband, children, the whole family thing. She'd never even tried, probably because her family had been so scattered, except now they weren't.

She glanced again at Rose and Sam; her brother had his arm around her, and she was cradling one of the babies. Violet was holding the other, inspecting her quite closely.

"I think she has a widow's peak, just like my father," she declared triumphantly.

What would it feel like, Seph wondered with a sudden, fierce surge of longing, to be like Rose and Sam, or Althea and John, or Will and Olivia? They'd all found love in coming back to Casterglass; could she find it, even though she'd never left? Did she even want to?

Making a friend had been scary enough. Daring to try for more was downright petrifying. In truth, she wouldn't even know where to begin.

And yet…

"I suppose I should get back to work," Oliver told her, startling her out of her jumbled thoughts. Rose was going to put the babies down for a nap, and everyone else was drifting away, back to whatever they had been doing before the big arrival. "I'm working on marketing today," he continued.

"I'm trying to convince Althea to run a Groupon deal but she's not sure about it."

"A Groupon deal? For what?"

"Two-for-one on candlelit ghost tours, led by your mother. I think she'd be fantastic, and she knows all the legends."

"That's true." Althea seemed discreetly determined to keep their slightly batty mother out of the way, but Seph saw how Violet could be an asset to the castle. "You should be thinking about things like this for Pembury," she told Oliver. "Not just Casterglass."

"Sadly, Pembury has no ghosts. But I might manufacture one. I'm sure I've heard some creaking in the attic on occasion, although it *might* just have been old plumbing."

"A ghost could definitely add some attraction," Seph agreed, smiling. "What would you name it?"

"Hmm." Oliver put his hands on his hips as he cast his eyes to the ceiling. "Male or female, do you think?"

"Why not both?" she suggested. "A lovelorn couple, even. They broke each other's hearts in life."

"And now reside in the same attic?"

She raised her eyebrows. "Maybe they found happiness in the afterlife?"

"A happy couple residing in the attic." He nodded slowly. "I like it. They could host tea parties."

Seph laughed and with one last quick grin and a salute, Oliver headed to the office while Seph decided to go back to her workshop. Yet as she walked slowly through the court-yard in a misting drizzle, she found she didn't want to work on yet another planter, or perhaps a cute sign for the garden or gift shop. The quaint but slightly kitschy stuff she'd been making so far had entertained her for a little while, but now she found herself longing for something more—in all sorts of ways.

She thought of how Oliver had told her how much he'd liked *Out of the Wild*, and how he thought she could exhibit artistic pieces, not just the run-of-the-mill useful stuff. She'd dismissed the notion almost immediately, because she didn't think she was that talented, and she wasn't even sure she wanted to exhibit anything so personal. It would be like tearing off bits of her soul and scattering them like confetti.

And yet...was this another way to try? To be? Once more she took the dust sheet off *Out of the Wild* and studied it critically. It had been challenging, in an invigorating sort of way, to meld the rough wood with the smooth, the untreated with the carefully sculpted, so the whole thing looked natural yet designed. Judging by Oliver's reaction, she had succeeded, and yet did she have any other inspiring ideas inside her?

She'd like to do something triumphant, Seph thought suddenly. Something victorious. Already an idea was forming in her mind, and she fumbled for a stub of pencil, a piece of paper, and began sketching, the lines bold and dark on the sheet.

"Seph?"

Seph jerked her head up to see her father, of all people, poking his head into her workshop. She didn't think he'd been in here once since she'd started. Quickly she stuffed the paper in her pocket and threw the sheet over her sculpture.

"Dad?" she asked. "Is something wrong?"

"Why should something be wrong?" he asked, smiling, although she thought he sounded slightly hurt. "I thought I'd visit you, to see how you were doing." Which happened just about never.

"Okay." She put her hand in her pockets and rocked back on her heels, waiting for something more. What had prompted this unexpected visit? Her father was smiling but Seph thought he looked a little uncomfortable as he glanced around her workshop.

"This is all quite remarkable," he said as he strolled slowly around. "I've seen your pieces in the gift shop, of course, and the garden, and I've been most impressed. But I should have come in here sooner, I think." He gave her a small smile that was touched with sorrow and felt, strangely, like an apology. An apology Seph had no idea what to do with.

"It's okay. I know you're busy."

"Not that busy." Her father let out a little sigh as he turned to face her. "I fear we might have neglected you, Persephone, over the years. Not intentionally, of course, but all the same." He shook his head slowly while Seph tried not to gape. Part of her wanted to sneer, *you think*. While another part, Oliver-style, wanted to assure him it was all okay, she'd been fine all along. She'd never seen her father look so...*sad*. She didn't like it.

"Have we?" he asked, meeting her stunned gaze directly. "I know you're a grown woman now, but when you were younger. Did you feel..." he swallowed "...abandoned?"

"Not...abandoned." Seph turned to her lathe, needlessly running a rag along its gleaming surface, just to have something to do. "Not quite."

Her father sighed again, more heavily this time. "I was afraid of that."

Her throat was getting thick as she squared her shoulders. "What's brought this on, anyway?" she asked.

"I suppose when you get to be my great age you start to look back on your life and re-evaluate," her father explained slowly. "And, admittedly, your siblings had something to say about their own situations."

"They did?" She hadn't realised anyone else had any real issues. But why, she wondered now, should she have assumed she was the only one? They'd all grown up at Casterglass, had had to deal with the castle's quirks, along with those of her parents. Admittedly, Althea, Olivia, and Sam had all had each other in a way she never had, but maybe they hadn't been as together as she'd thought. Maybe they'd had their own private struggles.

"We all have scars, I think," her father said. "It's part of the human condition. But it grieves me to think I may have had some part in causing yours."

Seph shook her head out of instinct, although she wasn't sure why. She was glad her father was saying this, but it also felt like too little, too late. Where had he or her mother been when she'd felt so lonely as a child, a teen? All the years of her childhood, basically fending for herself, from schooling to meals to endless school holidays on her own, kicking around the castle? Not that she'd ever said she wanted anything different. Not that she'd ever even complained.

"Your mother and I have been unorthodox in our parenting," her father continued. "Sometimes deliberately, to go against the grain, but sometimes out of—well, carelessness, I suppose. You always seemed so self-sufficient, even as a youngster, but you were still a child. Talking to your siblings has made me realise that I needed to talk to you, as well, and apologise for any hurts we might have caused." He looked at her seriously, then, so seriously and directly that Seph felt tears pooling in her eyes, thickening in her throat. She could not speak.

"Forgive me, Seph?" her father said quietly. "And your mother too? If we've hurt you? And not *if*, really. *When* we hurt you. Out of own thoughtlessness or selfishness."

Somehow, she managed to nod. Her father smiled, and then he put his arms around her in a gentle hug. Seph breathed in the familiar smell of him—leather and pipe tobacco and soil from his pottering about among his orchids. She closed her eyes and leaned into the hug in a way she never had before. It seemed she wasn't the only one who could be different, she thought as she eased back, surreptitiously wiping her eyes. She wasn't the only one who could try.

Chapter Twelve

"OLIVER, THIS IS fantastic."

Oliver tried not to beam too much as Althea clicked on the web pages he'd added to the castle's site. "Pick your own apples…cider making…even toddler craft sessions with apple printing and apple play dough! I didn't even know there was such a thing." She looked up, shaking her head in admiring wonder. "You've thought of everything."

"Well…" It had only taken a couple of clicks on Google, but he appreciated the admiration.

"Do you think the orchard will be ready for this autumn?" she asked. "Open for business?"

"Um, hopefully?" He was intending to prune them in January, via another YouTube tutorial, but by February he was hoping to be back at Pembury, with his uncle having made a decision. Autumn felt like a long time away.

"You've really been brilliant these last few weeks," Althea told him. "I don't know what I would have done without you."

"It was no trouble," Oliver assured her, even though it

occasionally had been.

It was mid-December, and only a week until Althea and John's wedding. As she'd become more involved—and stressed by—all the preparations, Oliver had taken over more and more of the daily running and admin. He'd liked feeling useful, as well as in charge, and since it was winter there wasn't too much to do, so he'd been able to organise her office as well as work on the website. He'd also made sure to file any invoice or bill as soon as it came in.

Yes, there had been a few annoyances, especially when she dumped some urgent bit of business in his lap at five minutes to five, but he'd managed. He'd even found the time in between jobs to stop and see Seph; he'd fallen into the habit of bringing her a coffee—a double-shot latte, her favourite—every afternoon. They'd sit in her workshop and chat for twenty minutes or so, before they both got back to work. It had never been about anything too serious, more a bit of joking and teasing, along with a rather epic and cutthroat Wordle competition. She'd got today's word in an impressive three, while Oliver had only managed four. All in all, he thought, it had been remarkably pleasant. More than pleasant, if he was honest.

Yesterday Seph had, rather shyly, confessed she was starting to work on another sculpture. "Just sketching," she'd said quickly. "Nothing in actual wood yet. But I don't think I would have thought of it on my own, so thank you for putting the idea in my head."

"I think you would have at some point," Oliver had replied. "But I'm glad to have been a help. I hope you're going to dedicate it to me when it's finished?" he'd teased, and she'd given a little laugh.

"Maybe."

They'd smiled at each other, and the moment had spun out a little long, as had been happening more and more frequently. There was an awareness growing between them, at least on Oliver's side. He wasn't sure whether Seph was having the same experience, but he found himself noticing things about her that drove him crazy, in an entirely wonderful way—the four freckles on her nose, and the way her golden curls clung to the back of her neck. How, when she stretched, her back always cracked, and she'd let out a little grimacing laugh before dropping her arms. When she was thinking, she scratched her nose, and when she was embarrassed, she lowered her gaze, so her lashes swept her cheeks. Yes, he'd spent a lot of time surreptitiously studying her. At least he hoped it was surreptitious.

"You know," Althea said, bringing him back to the present, "if you felt like it, you could stay on for a while. We could pay you a wage—not much, I admit, but something. You could work through the next year to get the orchard going? Be my right-hand man?" She smiled hopefully while Oliver simply stared, flummoxed.

He hadn't expected such an offer, and he wasn't sure what to do with it. Part of him wanted to leap at the chance to prove himself even more but also to stay at Casterglass and continue to get to know Seph. But another part thought longingly of Pembury, and he knew he needed to get back before the farm slipped through his fingers—although maybe it already had. The last text from his uncle had rather tersely informed him that he was taking Jack to Scotland for fly-fishing over Christmas, since 'the poor boy' worked so hard; Oliver clearly wasn't invited. Not that he cared—he didn't particularly like fishing—and there had been a fair few family holidays where he had not been included. Still, he'd been hoping to talk to his uncle about Pembury when he returned for Christmas. Now he wouldn't even be returning.

"I'll think about it," he told Althea, and she nodded briskly.

"Good. Please do. Now I'm afraid I have work to do—we've got some exciting plans ahead that I need to talk to Seph about." She gave a rather mysterious smile that had Oliver feeling a little alarmed. He was pretty sure Seph wasn't a fan of surprises.

"Exciting plans?" he asked neutrally. "Can I ask what they are?"

Althea gave him a rather narrowed look, and Oliver wasn't sure if he was overstepping, or she was wondering just what his interest was. He maintained what he hoped was a neutral, personable expression and waited for more.

"Just some developments on the property that will make Seph's life a little easier," she replied, with a mysterious smile that he suspected was meant to be quelling. "I'm sure she'll be thrilled."

With that, she rose and reached for her coat, leaving Oliver with no choice but to smile weakly. She'd be *thrilled*? He really wasn't so sure, and yet who was he to interfere? He'd come to know Seph pretty well over the last month, but he wasn't related to her. And yet as well-meaning as Althea could be, he still had an instinctive sense that she didn't really understand Seph.

Not the way you do.

Was it wrong, or worse, stupid, to think that way? To feel like he knew someone he'd met a month ago? As Althea left to impart whatever plans she'd been brewing, Oliver stared blankly at the computer screen, wondering what her news could be—and whether he should even care. He'd be leaving here in less than two months if he refused Althea's offer, which he felt he had to, for the sake of the farm.

And yet…for a second, he let himself imagine it. Living at Casterglass. Working to develop the orchard, the whole property. *Staying with Seph…*

He let out a sigh as the fantastical images evaporated in the ether of his mind. Casterglass wasn't his home, and considering how many Penryns there were already working here, he wasn't sure how people would take to him being Althea's right-hand man. And in any case, he wasn't sure that such a role didn't really mean her personal secretary. As for Seph…well, they were friends, certainly, but despite the awareness tingling through his whole body whenever he saw her, he didn't know how she felt. He'd misread signals before, if two years of dating could be reduced to *signals*. Did he really want to try again and be rebuffed? Laughed at? *Oh, Oliver, you didn't actually think…*

No, he didn't, particularly, thanks very much. Besides, there was Pembury to think of. Seph was never going to leave Casterglass; the place was in her bones, her blood. If he wanted to think about a future, it had to be with the farm, not the woman who occupied far too much of his thoughts.

❄

"SEPH? DO YOU have a moment?"

Seph looked up from the sketch she'd been working on, covering it quickly with her hand.

"Um, yes?" she said as Althea stepped into her workshop with her usual briskly efficient manner. "What's up?"

"I wanted to show you something." Althea's attitude was deliberately mysterious, which gave Seph pause. What plan was her sister hatching now? "Do you mind going for a walk?"

"No, I suppose not." Although her sister's manner was making her decidedly nervous. She didn't like surprises, but maybe Althea didn't realise that. As much as Althea was trying to get to know her now, there was still a twenty-year-gap in their relationship. "Let me just get my coat and boots," she said, and Althea nodded.

A few minutes later they were trudging through the

meadow that led to the sea, now a sea of clumpy mud, some frozen, some sludgy. As far as walks went, it wasn't the most picturesque; Seph had no idea where Althea was taking her so determinedly, marching through the field as if she had a GPS.

They skirted around the edge of Appleby Farm, heading for the single-track lane that cut through the far edge of the property, which dead-ended up at the beach.

"Where exactly are you taking me, Althea?" Seph asked as they finally clambered over a stile on the other side of the field, and landed on the lane.

"Here." She nodded towards three cottages huddled against the lane.

"Here?" Seph couldn't help but sound sceptical. The cottages had been built a hundred years or so ago, and had last been lived in in the 1980s, when they'd had casual labourers farming some of their fields. They looked seriously dilapidated now, and she suspected they were even worse inside. "Are you sure?"

"Yes, of course I'm sure." Althea brandished a key. "We can even go inside."

"Do we really want to?" Seph muttered under her breath as she followed her sister to the cottage on the far end, facing the sea. With a little jiggling and a judicious kick, Althea managed to unlock and open the door. The smell that wafted from the cottage's lounge was a mixture of mustiness and mildew that had Seph wrinkling her nose.

The place wasn't *quite* as bad as she thought; the furniture had been removed, and the wallpaper was hanging down in strips, but it could have been worse. There was a small, narrow lounge and a kitchen tacked onto the back; up a narrow set of stairs were two small bedrooms and a tiny bathroom. Back in the day, it probably would have housed a family of eight.

"Okay, so what's your big plan here?" she asked Althea. And what did it have to do with her?

"Well." Althea pushed her hair out of her eyes as she turned to Seph with a bright, determined smile. "We've got enough money now to do these cottages up. I had a look at them a while ago, and I was thinking about offering them as self-catering places, but then it occurred to me that really we could use them ourselves."

Seph glanced around the box-like living room with a decidedly dubious air. "Ourselves?"

"Yes...the castle is getting a little crowded, you know, with all of us home, and everyone with significant others now..."

"Not everyone," Seph reminded her, unable to keep a slight edge from her voice, and Althea nodded as if she'd made an extremely relevant point.

"That's right, not everyone."

Meaning not her. Everyone else was happily paired. Althea let out a little laugh, but Seph was already starting to feel wary.

"But you're moving to Appleby Farm," she pointed out. "So there will be a bit more space then."

"Yes, but Will and Olivia are thinking of moving into the castle after they're married—"

"They're not even engaged yet—" Seph protested.

"Only a matter of time," Althea assured her. "Olivia would like to live at Casterglass, and Will is quite open to it, as well. Once they fix up his cottage, they're thinking they'll sell it and move in. Their hope is to convert the top floor of the addition into a self-contained unit, a flat of sorts."

A whole floor? Her wariness was deepening into unease. "And what about Rose and Sam?" she asked after a moment.

"They want to do the same thing, with the first floor." Which is where Seph's bedroom was. "Mum and Dad have said they'll move into a downstairs room, and as you know the old part of the castle isn't really suitable to live in. It's freezing year-round."

"Yes." Seph had a feeling she knew where this was going, but she wanted her sister to say it.

"With the addition converted into flats, more or less," Althea continued briskly, "well, there's less space for everyone else. It makes sense, of course…families want their privacy. I can understand them all wanting their own space."

"Right." Seph took a deep breath. "So, the castle is going to be too crowded. Who are you thinking will live here?"

"Well…you, of course!" Was she imagining that Althea said that just a little too brightly? "We'd do it up, naturally. I think it could be quite cosy. And I imagine you want your privacy too—it's going to be very noisy, with all those little kids running around. And you are an adult, after all. I thought you'd like your own house..." Althea trailed off after a few moments when Seph had made no reply. "Seph?" she asked. "Don't you think it's a good idea?"

"Yeah, sure." Seph turned away, not trusting the expression on her face. Althea was acting as if Christmas had come early. Did she really believe that Seph would want to live in this grotty little place, one step up from a bedsit, miles from the castle, from anyone? To see her family, she'd have to trudge across several muddy fields. She'd be all by herself, all the time, while everyone else would be together, under one roof, a family. Was that what Althea thought she wanted? To be off on her own, isolated? She supposed it was the impression she'd given off over the years, and yet...

She was *trying* to be different. She thought everyone else was, too. But once again she had the depressing feeling that on a fundamental level, nothing had actually changed.

"Seph? What do you think?"

Seph stared out the small window at the view of the sea glinting greyly in the distance. The wind coming off the water would be ferocious, she thought, and for a second, she pictured herself huddled inside this little house, battered by the wind, entirely alone. It was enough to make her want to wince, weep, and give up all at once. That was not the life she wanted for herself. To live at Casterglass all of her days, alone, lonely, stuck in this cottage in the middle of no-where…yet what other future could she possibly have?

"Seph?" Althea asked again, and this time she sounded anxious.

Did her sister realise she'd got it wrong? Was she at least *wondering*? Or did she really think Seph would be happy here in her own space? Maybe she should be, Seph reflected. She'd lived most of her life virtually alone; why should Althea think anything different?

"Let me think about it," she said at last. "It's…quite a step."

"Yes, of course," Althea said quickly. "Perhaps I shouldn't have sprung it on you like this. I…I thought you'd be pleased."

Seph forced herself to turn around and face her sister. She knew Althea had meant to be kind, and it wasn't her fault that living in this little box of a cottage off on its own was now her idea of a worst nightmare. Maybe once, she reflected, she wouldn't have minded so much. Now she knew she did.

"I really appreciate the thought," she told her. "I…just need to think."

Althea nodded, a bit too much. "Yes, of course you do. Take all the time you want. I mean, within reason, of course. If you're going to move in, we'll need to get started on the renovations, especially if Rose and Sam want to start making changes up at the castle…" She trailed off uncomfortably while Seph made herself nod.

"Right. Yes. Within reason." She glanced out the window again. "What are you planning to do with the other two cottages?"

"Well...do them up eventually, maybe to let out? But we haven't got the money for those quite yet. Just this one."

"Ah." So, she really would be entirely alone out here.

Althea gazed at her for another few seconds, looking conflicted, a bit unhappy, like she wanted to say something more—and Seph realised she didn't want her to say it. She didn't want to continue this painful conversation, and she *really* didn't want to think about living in this poky little house all by herself.

"I should get back," she said, a bit abruptly. "And I'm sure you should, as well. You're getting married in just a week, after all!"

"Yes, crazy."

Althea shook her head, and Seph felt a pang of that old homesickness wash over her. Althea and John, Will and Olivia, Rose and Sam... She really was alone, whether she lived in this place or not.

And if she didn't live in this cottage, and Rose and Sam, Olivia and Will were taking over the castle...well, then maybe there wasn't a place for her at Casterglass anymore. And, she reflected glumly, there didn't seem to be a place for her anywhere else, either.

Chapter Thirteen

"CAN I SHOW you something?"

Oliver registered the hesitant note in Seph's voice and answered immediately. "Yes, of course you can. Have you been working on a sculpture?"

"No, nothing like that." She shook her head. "I mean, I have been, but this is something else altogether. Something I'd like your opinion on."

"Okay." Oliver regarded her closely, trying to figure out her mood. They were sitting in her workshop, having their usual coffee, and he'd sensed that Seph was a bit subdued, although he hadn't asked her about it. He'd wanted to wait for her to mention whatever it was that seemed to be getting her down, and now, maybe, she was about to. "Where is it, this thing you want to show me?" he asked. "Is it in here? Should we play twenty questions?"

She smiled at that, although he noticed it didn't reach her eyes. "No, it's on the other side of the property. You'll need your boots."

"Now I'm really intrigued." He wondered if this had anything to do with the exciting plans Althea had been developing, which she'd been so sure Seph would be thrilled about. That had been three days ago, and Seph certainly didn't seem thrilled now. "Shall I get my boots on now?"

"If you don't mind." She let out a small, defeated sigh that tore at his heart. Whatever was bothering her, he really hoped he could help.

Five minutes they were both suited up in winter coats and boots, heading across the field on the far side of the castle, that stretched all the way to the sea. It was a cold, grey afternoon, the kind of day when the sky felt as if it were pressing down on the world, and the sun was entirely hidden. Oliver buried his hands deeper into the pockets of his coat as he tucked his head low against the relentless wind from the sea.

"Is everything ready for the wedding, do you think?" he asked as they walked. He'd been spending most of his days either in the orchard or office, but he had seen people hurrying to and fro, and yesterday he'd accepted delivery of two dozen poinsettia plants for the great hall.

"I think so. Althea is like a whirling dervish, but I think she's mostly there. Ben and Poppy are coming back tomorrow, and I'm sure they'll help, too, and in any case it's a relatively small affair, isn't it? Only family and a very few close friends."

"True, although with a family this size…"

"Yes," Seph agreed, and gave another one of those dispirited sighs. "Exactly."

"So where are we going?" he asked, nodding towards the muddy fielding stretching out in front of them. "Because the answer to that appears to be the sea."

"Close to it," Seph agreed. "You'll see when you get there." She tucked her chin low and picked up her pace.

Ten minutes later they'd finally reached the end of the field and clambered over a stile to a single-track lane. There was nothing in sight but the sea and a couple of miserable-looking cottages right on the road.

"Those are something of an eyesore," Oliver remarked. "Do you think they'll be torn down?"

Seph let out a rather hollow laugh and then fished a key from her pocket. "No, unfortunately not," she replied, and then she went to the cottage on the end and unlocked the door.

With a growing sense of trepidation, Oliver followed her. Inside the place was dismal—musty, mildewy, the appliances in the kitchen a good fifty years old. Floorboards creaked as he walked across the tiny lounge to the three-bar electric fire in one wall, now full of mouse droppings.

"So," Seph asked, injecting a bright note into her voice that rang extremely false, "what do you think?"

Oliver turned slowly around in a circle as he took in the full dismalness of the room. "I think," he said after a moment, "that it's utterly awful."

Seph let out a bubble of laughter, but before Oliver had

even registered her, her expression collapsed, and she put her hands up to her face as her shoulders shook.

Shocked and appalled, Oliver took a few steps towards her. "Sorry, I didn't mean that—not...not exactly. It has potential, of course—"

She let out another shaky laugh as she shook her head. "No, it doesn't," she said through her fingers, and despite her sadness, he felt a wave of relief that he wasn't causing her tears. "It's horrible," she continued, her voice choking again. "Utterly horrible. I hate it."

"I think you're sensible, then." He took another cautious step towards her, longing to take her in his arms and comfort her, but not quite daring to. "Why did you bring me here?"

"Because Althea wants me to live here."

"What?" Oliver looked around again, appalled. The castle was shabby, it was true, but it was a grand, comfortable shabbiness, not like this little cottage, which just felt sad.

"She said I could do it up, of course," Seph continued, sniffing. "Within *reason*. But Sam and Rose and Will and Olivia are taking over the castle... They want to have their own self-contained flats, and so there won't be room for me." A sob escaped her, and her shoulders hunched.

"Oh, Seph." Oliver did put his arms around her then, and to his immense gratification, after only a second's startled pause, she leaned into him, resting her head on his shoulder as he stroked her back. "I'm sorry."

"The thing is," she continued after a moment, her voice

muffled against his shoulder, "I can't really blame Althea for thinking I'd want this. I've kept to my own company most of the time. I haven't been all that friendly or welcoming to her or to—to anyone. She seemed so pleased to be offering it to me, and I felt so…" she drew a shuddery breath "…sad."

"Oh, Seph," he said, his arms tightening around her just a little. She felt so soft and slender and right, he could have held her forever. "I really am."

She tilted her tear-stained face up to his. Teardrops clung to her lashes and her eyes were luminous. "*You* understand," she said, her tone caught between wondering and frustrating. "Why can't they?"

Because I've always understood you, Oliver wanted to say, but didn't. *Because I know you and I understand you and I might be falling in love with you.*

Thank goodness he didn't say any of that.

"Did you explain it to her?" he asked instead.

Seph slipped out of his arms, making him feel bereft. "No," she said on a sigh as she walked to the window, resting one hand on the frame. "I didn't feel I could, not when she was acting like she'd just given me the biggest birthday present ever. And, if I'm honest, I didn't want to have to. I wanted her to realise—what sort of person wants to be out here on their own, in this poky little place?" She shook her head slowly. "I imagined the rest of my life living here, and I just…couldn't bear it."

"I couldn't bear it either," Oliver said feelingly. "But I

suppose if it was done up nicely, it could be quite cosy. Maybe Althea was thinking along those lines?"

"Yes, while everyone else lived together at the castle?" Seph burst out bitterly. "Althea would be at Appleby Farm, I know, but it just...it just felt like I can't escape." She rested her forehead against the window frame and closed her eyes. "I've been alone my whole life and I don't want to be, anymore. I'm trying to be different, but maybe I can't be. Maybe nothing ever really can change, after all."

❄

SHE HADN'T MEANT to sound melodramatic, Seph thought as she kept her eyes closed, her forehead pressed against the window frame. She was afraid Oliver would think her terribly self-pitying, but Althea's suggestion had been stinging for three days. And not just the suggestion about this house, but everything. Last night she'd sat the supper table while everyone had chatted about the wedding and their Christmas plans, and she'd felt completely left out. Maybe that was her own making, but she couldn't escape the sense that everyone was so used to not including her that they didn't even think about it. They weren't *trying* to make her feel bad, and that knowledge actually made her feel worse.

Still, she was gratified Oliver understood. For a few seconds, when she'd rested in his arms, she'd felt...peaceful. That was really the only word to describe, even if the tingling sensation spreading through her body hadn't been exactly peaceful. But she'd felt as if she'd finally come to rest, as if she'd found a home, which was ridiculous, because it had only been a hug, born out of sympathy, nothing more.

Seph opened her eyes and raised her head from the window frame. "Sorry. I'm making more of this than there needs to be. I should just tell Althea I'm not interested. Even if Sam and Rose and Olivia and Will have their flats, I'm sure there will be room for me. I can take one of the pantries or something."

"You don't want to sleep in a pantry," Oliver pointed out wryly.

"You know what I mean, though." He was eyeing her with such gentleness that Seph had an urge to squirm. She'd cried in front of him. She'd cried in his *arms*. At the time it had felt wonderful and right, but now she was just embarrassed.

"Yes, I do." He spoke with a quiet certainty that made Seph want to ask *how* he knew, not just about this, but about everything. He seemed to understand her so well, and it surprised and scared and gratified her in turns. "You don't want people to be thoughtless, but pointing out that they've been thoughtless doesn't really help. You wanted them to have realised. To have cared."

"Yes." Once again, he'd encapsulated it perfectly. "But I do know that Althea cares," she continued, feeling it was important to be fair. "She'd made a lot of effort with the castle and with—with me. I wasn't very welcoming at all when she first came back." Seph squirmed inwardly to think about just how rude she had been. "And she tried. She still tries. So that's something."

"Do you want to live at the castle?" Oliver asked frankly. "And continue as things are? Or would you rather renovate something else—one of the stables, perhaps? You could still have your own space, but it would be a lot closer."

"Yes…" But as Seph tried to visualise turning the old dovecote or milking parlour into a cottage, she realised she didn't want that, either. Maybe *that* was what was at the heart of her jumbled hurt and confusion. "I don't…" she began, feeling her way through the words. "I don't really want to live at Casterglass at all."

"What?" Oliver looked so stunned that Seph would have laughed, if she hadn't felt so raw. Just saying that out loud had felt like a huge betrayal—of her family, her heritage, her very self.

"I don't want to live at Casterglass," she said again, more firmly this time because she realised she meant it. "I've lived here my whole life; I've never had a choice. You said it yourself—Casterglass is part of our family, not just like another person, but like—like a *king*, ruling over us all. It's in our bones, it's woven into the very fabric of our souls." She let out a self-conscious laugh. "I know how melodramatic that sounds, but I don't know how else to explain it."

Oliver was still looking flummoxed. "Why don't you

want to live at Casterglass?" he asked, still sounding shocked.

"I suppose because I've never known anything else. Because I've felt as if I've been hostage to this place—I didn't leave, and then I couldn't. I was afraid to, because I'd never known anything else. Before Althea came back, my dad was planning on selling it. When he told me, the first thing I felt was—relief." She bowed her head, almost ashamed by her confession. She'd never told this to another person; she'd never even let herself *think* it very much, in the privacy of her own mind.

"I had no idea," Oliver replied slowly.

"Are you disappointed?" she asked, although she wasn't quite sure why he would be. "It feels wrong, like I should love it because it's our home, and it is so wonderful in many ways, but everyone else got to leave. I never did." She thought of her siblings traipsing off to boarding school, to university, to cheap and cheerful holidays with friends in Portugal or Spain. Sam had been all over the world; Althea had worked in London and Olivia in York. She'd done nothing, *nothing* in comparison.

"I've always wanted to travel," she admitted impulsively. "Go to Europe—Paris or Prague or, I don't know, *somewhere*. Sit in a café and watch the world go by. Wander city streets late at night." She blushed, knowing how fanciful she sounded. "I've never done anything like that, not even remotely. The only times I've left Cumbria were for Olivia's graduation and a sixth form school trip to Lancaster." A trembling laugh escaped from her lips. "I bet you can't even believe that, in this day and age. I've never even been to London."

"Your parents never travelled with you?"

"By the time I came along, they were happy to just potter about here. Everyone came to us, that is, when they did. As time went on, they didn't come back all that much. But there were some fun times..." Again she felt she had to be fair. "Parties and things, especially when I was younger. I remember an epic croquet match that went on till about two in the morning."

"So, everyone else has been coming home, finding their place," Oliver surmised slowly, his head cocked as his gaze swept thoughtfully over her, "and you were desperate to leave and find your place somewhere else."

"I suppose," Seph replied, once again feeling her way through the words, the emotions. "I don't want to be tied to a place anymore. Any place. Beholden to a pile of bricks and mortar, so your whole life revolves around it. I want to experience things—I want to *live* a little, more than I have, anyway. Try new things. Be daring. Explore." She laughed, pressing her hands to her hot cheeks. "I didn't realise I was going to say all that. I'm not even sure I knew I felt it." She shook her head, embarrassed but also relieved. It had felt good to admit it all. Good and even important to acknowledge it to herself, never mind to Oliver or anyone else. "Everyone thinks I'm a homebody," she finished, "but I want the chance to see if I'm not one, after all."

Oliver nodded slowly. "I can understand that," he said after a moment. There was a tinge of sorrow to his voice that made Seph anxious.

"Do you think I'm crazy? Or selfish? Or—"

"Seph, I don't think you're anything but wonderful." He met her gaze directly and the warmth in his eyes, the sincerity in his tone, made her feel jolted, as if she'd stuck her finger or really her whole body into an electrical socket. Everything was suddenly alight. Blazing.

"You—do?" she asked uncertainly.

"Yes, I do." He sounded firm and matter-of-fact in a way that made her smile. How could he be so sure? And yet, wonderfully, he was. She opened her mouth to tell him that she thought he was wonderful too, but somehow she just couldn't find the courage. In any case, Oliver didn't give her much opportunity.

"Now, come on," he said, holding out his hand so she felt she had to take it, which was no bad thing at all. The slide of his palm against hers thrilled her, just as it had the last time she'd taken his hand.

"We've spent enough time in this hovel," he declared with a smile. "Let's walk back to the castle by the beach rather than through that muddy field." He waggled his eyebrows as he gave her a teasing, mischievous look. "If you want to experience things, well, there's no time like the present, is there?"

Chapter Fourteen

T HE SKY HAD cleared to a paler grey with wisps of blue visible through the clouds as Oliver and Seph walked along the lane towards the beach. Oliver's head was buzzing with everything Seph had told him—he felt like throttling Althea, but he also felt like groaning aloud. *I don't want to be tied to a place anymore. Any place. Beholden to a pile of bricks and mortar, so your whole life revolves around it.*

Well, it didn't get much clearer than that, did it? Seph had sounded so passionate when she'd told him that, and Oliver's incredulous hope that she would be willing to leave Casterglass—if it ever came to that, for them, which admittedly was a long way off—had suddenly crumbled to dust. If she didn't want to be tied to Casterglass, she wouldn't want to be tied to the far more modest Pembury.

Except why was he even thinking that way? They weren't dating, even if they'd become friends. Good friends, *really* good. Still, it was a long way from asking someone to spend her life with you, and yet…

Oliver knew that was the way he was starting to think.

To hope and to long for, because the time he spent with Seph was precious and sweet, and he didn't want to give it up. He wanted more of it, lots more. He thought of how she'd felt so briefly in his arms, and he knew he wanted a lot more of that, too.

Was he crazy to think she might, as well? When he'd told her she was wonderful, she'd looked astounded, but also pleased. But, Oliver reminded himself, she hadn't said he was wonderful back, or even okay or merely adequate. She hadn't said anything at all, which was why he'd decided to move the conversation on, before it got too awkward and he jumped in and said all sorts of things he knew she wasn't ready for, because that was the way he tended to operate.

Seph was looking lost in thought as they walked along, and while the silence was companionable, Oliver felt the need to *do* something. She'd said she wanted to experience things, to live life to the full and all that jazz—well, he wanted to help her. Why not start now?

They'd come to the end of the lane, which tapered off into a sandy track that led right down to the sand. The tide was out, so the little cove was a smooth sweep of damp, golden sand, the frothy waves lapping the now-distant shore, the air clear and cold. Very cold.

Oliver stopped where he stood.

It took Seph a few moments to clock he'd stopped, and she turned back to face him, eyebrows raised. "What is it?" she asked. "Why are you staring out at the sea like that?"

Oliver turned to her. "Let's go swimming."

"Swimming?" She goggled at him, understandably. "Oliver, it's freezing. It's also almost Christmas. In Cumbria. Are you *crazy*?"

He shrugged, smiling, determined, filled with a sudden, surging lightness, almost like joy. Maybe he was crazy. "Maybe, probably?" he said. "But you know what they say about wild swimming...how invigorating it is. Who is that guy who swears by sub-zero temperatures?" She shook her head slowly, still disbelieving. "Wim Hof, that's who. I've watched his YouTube videos."

"I've never heard of him."

"Well, if you'd had, you'd be impressed. He's like a real-life superman. He's got a six-pack at sixty years old, and he's all about the amazing benefits of cold therapy—like, sitting on an iceberg for three hours or something."

"Sounds fun," Seph returned drily, and Oliver grinned.

"Don't worry, there are no icebergs here. Let's have a quick dip, to wake up all your senses." With a heady sense of recklessness, enjoying the moment, he unzipped his coat.

Seph's eyes widened. "Are you...*stripping*?"

"Down to my boxers, yes," he replied with far more confidence than he actually felt, while she goggled all the more. "I will remain modestly clothed, I assure you."

"You'll catch your death of cold—"

He arched an eyebrow as he shucked off his coat. "I thought you wanted to live a little?"

"Not by starting with a death wish!" She shook her head, exasperated now, but a smile was flirting with her lips and Oliver thought he could convince her. He hoped so, considering he was taking off his clothes. It would be rather embarrassing to have to swim alone. What madness had gripped him, he wasn't even sure, because he didn't particularly enjoy swimming even in the mildest of weather. As for the middle of winter...

But it would be with Seph. And he wanted to wake her up, take her out of her comfort zone, to help her to do just what she'd said she wanted to do—live a little. He pulled off his jumper. "Are you in or not?"

She glanced askance at the grey-blue waves; the wind coming off the sea was pretty arctic, so he didn't even want to imagine how cold the water actually was. Hopefully neither of them would catch pneumonia or go into shock or something horrible like that. He pictured giving her CPR right there on the beach and suppressed a shudder of fear. It would be fine, just a quick dip. A really quick dip.

"All right, fine." She tossed the words at him with a defiance that made him smile. "But let's do it quickly."

"Absolutely."

He undressed right down to his boxers, embarrassed suddenly by showing so much skin, although he knew it was more or less the same as wearing a swimsuit. Still, it was more of his flesh than Seph had ever seen before, wintry white and coming out in goose pimples. Not the most attractive look, but…

"All right, I'm ready." He turned and saw that Seph had undressed down to her vest top and underpants, her arms wrapped around her body as she shivered. Her legs were endless and golden, her body slender and perfect. Oliver wondered if this whole endeavour had just been a way his subconscious had thought of to see more of her. She was so beautiful, everything in him ached. *Everything.*

"All right, let's go." He reached for her hand and with a shy smile she took it. "On the count of three?"

She nodded, and they both turned to the water. It looked really rather cold. Like, seriously cold.

"One…" Seph squeezed his hand. "Two…" Even tighter. "*Three!*"

She ran first, pulling him along, her long legs galloping over the damp sand as she headed straight for the water, so Oliver had no choice but to sprint to keep up with her. She didn't hesitate for a second as she splashed through the shallows, but good Lord, it was truly freezing. Within seconds he couldn't feel his toes. His ankles were *burning*, which was an odd sensation considering how cold the water was, but that was how it felt. Like his body was on icy fire.

Then his calves were burning, and then his knees, his thighs, his—He was going to die. This really was going to kill him. Seph would have to drag him out of the water. Wim Hof was a sadist, and he must have been mad to suggest such an absurd, ridiculous, insane, dangerous thing to do—and yet Seph pulled him deeper into the icy water.

"Come on." She laughed, and then he watched as she dove under water and came up again, sluicing the water from her face as if she were a mermaid frolicking in the sea. "You're right, it is invigorating!" she called out to him. Oliver's teeth were chattering too much to reply.

"Aren't you going to go under?" she teased, and somehow he forced himself to do it, even though everything in him resisted the icy torture. So. Cold. That was all he could think of, his body burning, his head pounding, until he rose from the water and turned to see Seph standing waist-deep in the sea, happily oblivious to the fact that her vest top was plastered to her body and completely see-through. Oliver prided himself on being something of a gentleman, and so he averted his gaze, but not before he'd got a delicious eyeful.

Goodness but she was beautiful—and brave. He felt as if he'd seen a glimpse of the woman she could truly be, if given the opportunity, the courage. She was brave and beautiful, bold and strong, ready to scoop up all life had to offer with both hands. He really was falling in love with her, he thought with a ripple of incredulous wonder. Could it happen that fast? Could he trust his feelings?

"I *am* freezing," Seph told him as she started to wade out of the water.

Oliver followed her, doing his best not to shiver uncontrollably as they yanked on their clothes over their frigid, goose-pimpled skin.

"I think this calls for hot chocolate by the fire when we get back," Seph said, to which Oliver offered his heartfelt agreement. Cosying up by a roaring fire was, he realised, much more his style than swimming in ice water, as invigorating as it had been. Every nerve was tingling, certainly.

As they headed down the path towards the wood, Seph gave him a small, hesitant smile. "Thank you," she said quietly. "That was brilliant."

"You got into the spirit of it admirably," Oliver replied. "Better than I did, certainly."

She laughed. "Your lips are still blue."

"I'm not surprised."

She shook her head, still smiling, and they walked in easy silence all the way back to the castle.

❄

SEPH COULDN'T REMEMBER the last time she'd felt so...*happy*. And not just happy, but full of joy and wonder. She would have never imagined that a simple swim could create such a sense of euphoria, but she knew it wasn't just because of the water, no matter how Wim Whoever extolled the benefits of cold therapy. She was happy because she was with Oliver, because he seemed to see something in her that no one else ever had, because being with him made her laugh and tease and dream, and it was all so wonderfully liberating, she felt like a new person.

She wished she could tell him something of how she felt,

but she didn't have the words and she worried it would sound like too much. *Thank you for helping me come alive.* It wasn't the kind of thing anyone said, outside of some sappy romcom. And yet she wanted to say it; she wanted him to know.

"Whoa, what happened to you?" Will stood in the kitchen by the kettle, his eyes wide as he took in their wet hair and damp clothes. Oliver's lips still held a bluish tinge. "Who fell in, and who came to the rescue?"

"We went wild swimming," Seph told him with a blithe recklessness. "It was amazing. You should try it, Will."

"You went swimming in the sea in December?" Will's eyes rounded. "And you haven't caught pneumonia?"

"Not yet," Oliver replied. "But I'll let you know in a few days. I still can't feel my toes."

"Go change," Seph told him with a laugh. "I'll make the hot chocolate."

"You need to change too," Oliver pointed out, and she shrugged.

"I can survive for a few minutes. I'll bring it upstairs, to the sitting room."

Oliver looked as if he wanted to object, probably out of chivalry, but then he shivered and nodded. "All right. Thank you."

After he'd left, Will gave Seph a curious, considering look. "You two seem to have hit it off."

"We have," Seph replied firmly, surprising not just Will

but herself. In the past she would have backtracked—or bitten his head off. She really was changing.

"That's great, Seph," Will said as he poured milk into his tea. "I'm glad."

"I am too," she replied simply, and Will hefted his mug in a toast before he ambled off to the garden. Seph made two cups of hot chocolate, complete with lashings of whipped cream and heaped with marshmallows, and then she brought them upstairs. Oliver was still changing, and so she left the mugs on a table and hurried to change herself, humming all the while. It felt strange to be this happy, and yet she was.

By the time she returned to the sitting room, dressed in a warm fleece and jeans, Oliver had just kindled a cheering blaze in the fireplace.

"Ah, perfect!" he exclaimed, his face lighting up when he saw her. "A fire, hot chocolate, dry clothes…what more can a person ask for?"

He handed her one of the mugs and then hefted his own, proffering it for a clinking toast before they both took sips of the rich, warming drink.

"I didn't expect to like wild swimming so much," Seph confessed as she curled up in an armchair on one side of the fireplace, and Oliver sat in the other. "I really did think you were a bit mad to suggest it."

"I thought I was a bit mad myself," Oliver replied cheerfully. "Especially after we'd made it into the water. I have to confess I think Wim Hof is a deluded fool, six-pack aside."

She laughed, the sound bubbling up inside her. "So I guess you won't be accompanying me again?"

"You intend to go again?" He raised his eyebrows. "Have I started something?"

"Maybe," she replied nonchalantly, wondering if they were flirting. She had so little experience with this sort of thing that she really didn't know.

"Well, I might be convinced," Oliver replied slowly. The look he gave her was...loaded. Or at least, it *felt* loaded. She felt...something. Seph buried her nose in her mug, because she had no idea what the expression on her face was. Her whole body was tingling, and this time it was definitely not from the cold.

"Maybe when you come back after Christmas," she said, and Oliver's momentary pause forced her to look up from the depths of her drink. "What?" she asked uncertainly.

"Nothing," he answered quickly. "I mean, yes. After Christmas."

She eyed him narrowly, noting the sudden downturn of his mouth, the shadow in his eyes. "You're going back to Pembury Farm for Christmas, aren't you?" she asked.

"Er, well. I suppose." He let out an uncertain, little laugh. "My uncle and cousin are going fly-fishing in Scotland for the holidays. So if I go back to Pembury, it will be by myself, which actually would be okay, but my uncle can be a bit funny about having people there without him."

"But it's your home," Seph said in surprise. Even though

Oliver had said something of his tricky relationship with his uncle before, she'd assumed he was always welcome at the house he loved so much.

"Well, yes. Sort of. I mean, I certainly feel it is." He sighed and shook his head. "It doesn't matter."

But she had the sense that it really did. "You could stay here for Christmas," she said slowly, and Oliver raised his eyebrows in surprise.

"I don't think I should intrude on a family celebration—"

Seph let out a hollow laugh. "Haven't you heard the plans? There isn't going to be one."

"What do you mean?"

He must have missed that conversation, she realised, being so busy with the orchard and all the other things, now that Althea was consumed with planning her wedding. "No one will be here for Christmas," she explained. "No one but me, that is. My parents are going on an over-sixties cruise, and Rose and Sam are visiting her mother. Will and Olivia are spending Christmas with his parents, and Althea and John are, of course, going on honeymoon." She shrugged, like it didn't matter, when, just like with him, she knew it did. "Everybody's got plans."

"So you'll be on your own?"

"Yes, but I'm used to it." She tried to say it matter-of-factly, without bitterness. It was true, even if she had started to wish it wasn't.

"For Christmas?" Oliver shook his head slowly. "Didn't

anyone think about what you would do?"

"My parents offered for me to accompany them on their cruise, but I don't want to cramp their style, and spending a week with a bunch of bingo-playing pensioners...well, it could be worse, I suppose, but I don't really fancy it."

"And what about everyone else?"

She shrugged. "I'm not a child, and they're all in their thirties and forties. It's not their job to think about me that way." Something she had started to realise, after feeling like the forgotten child for so long. She was a grown woman now, in charge of her own life. "Maybe I'll go to Paris," she told Oliver with the same nonchalance she'd spoken with earlier. "Or Prague. Spend Christmas in a strange city by myself." She knew she wouldn't.

"You should," Oliver told her. "That is, if you really want to."

Seph put her mug down and hugged her knees to her chest. "I don't really know what I want," she admitted. "I've spent my whole life here, and sometimes it's felt like a prison, but I'm too afraid to go out and do something, all by myself." She bit her lip, embarrassed by admitting so much. This whole vulnerability thing had become a bit easier, but it still felt hard. "You could spend Christmas here, if you wanted," she told him, not wanting to sound too desperate and yet feeling it. Wanting him to, so much. "It could be fun, even if it would just be the two of us rattling around." Which did sound fun, to her, but Oliver had a distant look on his face like he was thinking about other, more attractive possibilities.

"I could," he said slowly, but he didn't sound remotely convinced. *Ouch.*

She'd been practically begging him to, Seph realised with a scorching flush of shame. She jumped up from her seat, whisking their mugs away. "We should get going," she said, ducking her head so she didn't have to look at him. "I'm sure Althea has a list a mile long of things for you to do, and I'm meant to be finishing some table favours she has me making. Little wooden pots—"

"Seph, I didn't mean I didn't want to spend Christmas here—" Oliver began, but she shook her head, speaking over him.

"No, no, it's fine. Christmas isn't really that much of a thing in my family anyway. I mean, we usually get a tree and there are a few presents, but until last year it was all pretty hit or miss. I don't mind being here on my own, honestly." Somehow, she forced herself to look at him and smile, although she couldn't quite look him in the eye. "We should get going," she said again, and then she hurried from the room, wanting to hide her hurt and embarrassment from him, even if she couldn't hide it from herself.

Chapter Fifteen

I T WAS POURING rain, which suited Oliver's mood perfectly. He gazed gloomily at his reflection in the age-spotted mirror in his tiny bedroom under the eaves, as rain drummed on the roof and the front lawn became a sea of mud. It was the day of Althea's wedding, and everyone was flying around the house, creating a happy chaos as they finished all the urgent, last-minute things—flowers to arrange or deliver, table favours to assemble, bridesmaid dresses that needed emergency alterations.

Oliver had been on the periphery of it all; he'd offered to help, but he seemed only to be getting in the way, and so he'd retreated to his bedroom to put on his jacket and tie in preparation for the evening ceremony. It was meant to be a small, intimate wedding for immediate family and local friends, with a candlelit ceremony in the parish church in Casterglass, and then a reception in the great hall back at the castle. Oliver felt a bit like a pretender, being here at all, when he'd only known the family for less than two months, but they'd insisted he stay for the wedding.

As for what came after…

Oliver grimaced at his reflection before turning away. He'd made a real mess of that. When Seph had suggested he stay at Casterglass for Christmas, he'd been both touched and thrilled, of course he had, but he knew he hadn't acted like it—only because he'd been thinking about something else! Something better. But did he dare suggest such a thing to Seph?

In any case, she hadn't given him the opportunity. In the three days since they'd had that conversation, she hadn't been avoiding him, not exactly…but close. Very close. When he'd taken her a coffee to her workshop, she'd thanked him and then fired up her lathe, explaining she was busy. When he'd tried to have a chat after dinner or in one of the infrequent lulls in the daily grind, she'd been friendly enough but hurried away pretty darn quickly, with the excuse she had to do something for Althea. And things *had* been busy, with everyone going into pre-wedding hyperdrive. He couldn't blame her for that, and yet he sensed instinctively that she was avoiding him for a reason—because he hadn't jumped on the chance of spending Christmas with her at Casterglass.

Which was *stupid*, because of course he wanted to spend Christmas with her. He'd just never got an opportunity to tell her so, although in all honesty Oliver knew that was as much his fault as Seph's. They both had a terror of putting themselves out there, he thought, they just handled it in different ways. But Christmas was in five days, and everyone was leaving Casterglass in the next forty-eight hours. It was make-or-break decision time. The question was—did he have the guts?

Recklessly Oliver reached for his laptop. Unfortunately, the Wi-Fi signal was too weak to reach his bedroom up in the attic, so he took it downstairs to the sitting room, which was thankfully empty as everyone was taking photographs. The wedding was in less than an hour, the calm before the storm. Oliver opened his laptop, pressed a few buttons. Could he really do this? Was he presuming too much? Would Seph be annoyed or even appalled?

And yet...

They'd both spent their life on the fringes of family, living in the shadows and pretending they liked it. Seph had acted indifferent and sullen, while he'd tried too hard to be cheerful and easy to please. Two sides of the same sad coin, but they could be different now. Different together.

In a different place...

Drawing a deep breath, Oliver clicked the mouse of his laptop, and then released his breath in a shuddery sigh as he saw it had gone through. The die was cast. Now he just had to work up the courage to ask Seph.

"Oliver, there you are!" Violet wafted into the room in a surprisingly staid dress of royal blue to whose neckline she had attached several garish, fake blowsy red roses. "Althea wanted you in some of the photos."

"What?" Oliver stared at her, appalled. He was little

more than an acquaintance, far from family. "I don't think—"

"Oh, come on, now," Violet said with a playful smile. "You are practically family, you know."

"Not really—"

"Well, who knows, you might be one day." While Oliver merely gaped, she continued blithely, "I'd almost think there was something in the water, the way people have been pairing off."

"Um…" Oliver had no idea what to say to any of that.

"You don't need to say a word, dear boy," Violet told him with an airy smile, "it's all there in your face, and has been for some time. And in Persephone's face, as well, I might add. I rather think you are perfect for each other. Hopefully over Christmas you'll stop dithering about it."

Oliver felt a flush fight its way up his neck and suffuse his face. Had all the Penryns been talking about him and Seph? The thought was utterly mortifying.

"I don't know what's happening over Christmas," he said, despite his recent activity on his laptop.

Violet raised her thin, pencilled eyebrows. "Don't you? I assumed you were spending it with my daughter."

"Why would you assume that?" Oliver asked dumbly.

"Because she's alone and so are you." Violet shook her head slowly. "If you think I am the sort of person who has any interest in going on a cruise for over-sixties, then you are quite mistaken. I have never played bingo in my life, and I do not intend to start."

Wait, they'd *planned* it? They'd left Seph on her own in the hope that he'd, what, take *pity* on her? "But how did you know I'd be alone, too?" he asked.

Violet's expression turned gentle as she gave him a smile touched with pity. "Dear Oliver," she said, "it's written all over you."

Stung, Oliver could only blink. Did he come across that much as a loner? Pathetic, even? Jeez, Violet knew how to deliver a zinger. "I was supposed to go back to Pembury Farm," he said, and Violet just smiled and shook her head.

"Now come along," she told him, reaching for his elbows and steering him out of the room as if he were about six. "For the photos. And the ceremony, of course."

Everyone was assembled downstairs in the great hall, which had been bedecked with swathes of mistletoe, holly, and winter roses, as well as dozens of poinsettias. Instinctively, without even realising he was doing it, he searched for Seph—and found her, standing by Olivia, looking...well, enchanting was one word. Stunning was another. He gaped at her before he remembered to close his mouth, and then he tried to affect an expression that was not quite so gormless.

She was wearing a dress in forest-green velvet that skimmed her slender body and swirled about her ankles. Her hair was in its usual ringlets, with a crown of white roses. She carried a matching posy of roses, and she looked like something out of Shakespeare or Jane Austen or even a fairy tale, ethereal and lovely and just, well, perfect.

"All right, everyone together!" the photographer called out, and everyone jostled for position. Oliver tried to move closer to Seph, but found himself steered towards the back, where he stood next to Will.

"She looks beautiful, doesn't she?" he whispered, and then winked.

Okay, did everyone know he had a thing for Seph? It seemed so, and that made Oliver feel very…exposed. Especially since Seph had been avoiding him for three days. Then he remembered what he'd planned and recklessly thought screw it. He didn't care if he seemed exposed, or if everyone knew. He was going to tell Seph how he felt. He was going to ask her to spend Christmas with him. If it wasn't coming as a surprise to her family, perhaps it wouldn't to her, either.

❄

THE CHURCH LOOKED lovely, its pews swathed in holly and roses, candles twinkling and shimmering everywhere. Nerves fluttered in Seph's stomach as she stood at the top of the aisle, about to process down after Olivia, to the lovely strains of Pachelbel's "Canon." There were only about thirty people in the congregation, which made it easy to spot Oliver. He was on the bride's side, the third row from the front, trying to meet her gaze but she was doing her best not to look at him.

All right, she was a coward. She knew that. After feeling so happy and confident and free, her newly minted self had collapsed into uncertainty, all from Oliver's single lukewarm response. *I could*, he'd said, like he was thinking of ten other things he'd rather do, and the people he'd rather do them with.

Maybe it was unreasonable, to let a single moment affect her so much, but the changes she'd been making were so recent and raw, they couldn't bear the weight of her crisis in self-confidence, as she'd quickly discovered. And Oliver hadn't exactly tried to make up for that moment, had he? He hadn't broached the subject of Christmas again, which had confirmed her unhappy suspicions that he didn't want to spend the holiday with her.

Which was fine, she told herself, uselessly, over and over again. They could still be friends. Spending Christmas together had been a step too far; that was all. If she had more confidence, she would have said something of this to him— laughed it off, told him he didn't need to panic, he could do what he liked. She could have acted indifferent, the way she used to, that trusty armour of self-protection that was defeating her now, because once she'd disassembled it, she struggled to know how to put it back on.

"Seph...go!" Rose nudged her in the back, and she took a slightly stumbling step down the aisle before thankfully righting herself and continuing on, chin up, eyes straight ahead. *Don't look at Oliver...don't look...*

She didn't.

THE CEREMONY WAS, of course, beautiful. John and Althea looked perfect together, the four children between them all beaming, the guests smiling or becoming teary-eyed or both. The rain drumming on the roof only added to the beauty somehow. Nothing could spoil their day, Seph thought as Althea and John began the exchange of rings, not when they were so clearly in love with each other.

"I give you this ring," John said to Althea, his voice hoarse with emotion as he slid the ring on his bride's finger. "As a symbol of my vow, and with all that I am and all that I have I honour you…"

All right, now Seph was feeling a bit emotional. A lump was forming in her throat, an ache of happiness for her sister and longing for herself. She wanted those words, she thought. She wanted someone to feel that strongly about her, to love and cherish and honour her, to make promises meant to last for the rest of their lives…

Without even realising she was doing so, she turned to look at Oliver—and discovered, with a startled jolt, that he was looking right at her. His hazel eyes blazed gold and green as he looked at her and she looked back, and for a few seconds everything and everyone else faded away, and it was just the two of them, and their locked gazes.

Then Oliver offered a smile—tentative, shy, tender. Her lips trembling, Seph smiled back.

"I now declare you husband and wife."

The congregation erupted in cheers as John took the opportunity to give his wife a hearty kiss. Startled, Seph broke Oliver's gaze and did her best to smile and clap, even as everything in her wondered and reeled.

Had she been imagining the intensity of that look? Longing for it, because of how she'd been feeling? She had no idea, and she was afraid to try to find out.

In any case, there was no opportunity to talk to Oliver in the crush after the service, and then the logistics of getting everyone back to the castle in the pouring rain. By the time Seph had made it in the back of Will's Land Rover, slightly damp and crumpled, the party was in full swing, and she couldn't see Oliver anywhere, which maybe was just as well.

She got herself a glass of champagne and skirted the great hall, smiling and nodding at those she passed without engaging too much, which was easy enough, although it left her feeling restless. Everyone would be leaving in a few days, and she would be knocking about this castle, entirely alone. She had no idea where Oliver would go, wasn't brave enough to ask—

"There you are."

Seph whirled around to find Oliver smiling at her crookedly. He cleaned up nicely in a blue blazer and crimson tie, his usual rumpled cords replaced with a pressed pair of chinos.

"I hope you haven't been avoiding me," he said, and Seph opened her mouth to say, somewhat scornfully, 'of course not', when something else came out instead.

"Actually, I have."

Oliver raised his eyebrows. "Because of what I said about Christmas?"

It was, strangely and surprisingly, a relief that he was going to state it as plainly as that. "More what you didn't say, I suppose," Seph replied. Her tone was matter-of-fact, but she could feel herself blushing.

"All right. Yes. What I didn't say." Oliver nodded, and Seph saw he was starting to blush, as well. "But what I should have said, is that I'd love to spend Christmas with you, and in fact, unless you've made other plans, I'm hoping to."

There was something so endearingly nervous about his tone, his expression, and yet something wasn't quite computing. "You mean...you're staying at Casterglass?" she asked.

"No. That is...I could, but I thought...maybe..." Oliver let out a little, strangled laugh. "I might have taken something of a liberty," he told her. "Because—well, because I wanted to, I guess."

"A liberty?" Seph had no idea what he was talking about.

"I booked a flight," he said in a rush. "And a hotel. And dinner on Christmas Day, and a performance of *The Nutcracker*. But that's it, I promise."

Seph could only stare. "What?" she finally asked blankly, when he seemed to be expecting a response. "What are you talking about?"

"You said you wanted to travel, to go to Paris or Prague,"

he explained nervously. "Well, I think Paris is a bit overrated, and I've always wanted to go to Prague. So I booked us a trip, over Christmas. Three days in Prague. We leave on the twenty-third."

"What…" The word escaped Seph in an incredulous breath. "You did?" she finally said, because even though he'd just said it all, she still couldn't believe it. "You booked a whole trip?"

"Yes. Non-refundable, too, because I booked it so late, so I'm really hoping you meant what you said, and you actually do want to go to Prague."

"I…I do," Seph said. "So…we'd go together?"

For a second something flickered across Oliver's face, and it took Seph a second to realise it was hurt. It was the same expression she suspected had been on her face when he'd answered her invitation with *I could*, in such a dubious way.

"Well, yes, that was the idea," he answered after a pause. "But, ah, if you'd rather go alone—"

"I wouldn't." She wanted to be clear, wonderfully clear. "I wouldn't at all. I…I want to go with you, Oliver. A lot."

The grin that spread across his face was wonderful to see. Seph let out a sudden, awed laugh, as realisation rushed through her. She was going to Prague! *They* were!

"Well, that's really good," Oliver said, "because I want to go with you. You do have a passport, right? I didn't even think to check."

"Yes, although I've never actually used it." There had been talk of a family trip to France a few years ago that had never come to anything.

"Good, phew. Then we really can go. We're staying at a hotel right off the Charles Bridge—probably really touristy and naff, but I don't know any better."

"It sounds perfect."

"And, ah…" He tugged at his collar, his face reddening again. "We have to share a bedroom, because of the expense, but of course there are separate beds. I mean, obviously. I hope that's okay. The shared room, I mean, not the—not the bed thing."

"Yeah, sure, of course." Seph nodded, not looking at him, her own face turning scarlet. What did he mean, obviously? I mean, yes, she agreed, they weren't even dating so sharing beds would be weird, but still. Why *obviously*?

"Okay." Oliver blew out a breath. "Good. Great."

"Yes. Great."

They were still staring at each other as Olivia swooped down on them. "Hey, you two! As neither of you are doing anything, would you mind holding a couple of babies so Rose and Sam can dance?" Without further ado, she plopped Bea into Seph's arms, and Michaela into Oliver's. At least, she thought she was holding Bea. She still couldn't tell them apart.

She cuddled the baby close as Rose and Sam took the floor.

"Their heads are still so *floppy*," Oliver said, sounding alarmed, and Seph let out a little laugh of pure joy. They were going to Prague. And who knew what might happen there? The world felt as if it were brimming and shimmering with possibility.

"Oh no," Oliver said, sounding even more alarmed. "I think this one might have filled her nappy."

Chapter Sixteen

"WELCOME TO PRAHA, the city of a thousand spires!" As Seph stepped off the aeroplane, she felt a rush of excitement—and nervousness. They'd actually done it. They'd gone to Prague.

The last few days had been a whirlwind, as everyone had prepared to go on their separate Christmas trips. Seph had half-hoped she might fly under the radar, but of course that hadn't happened. Olivia had passed by her bedroom and seen her packing and had immediately wanted to know where she was going.

"I thought you were staying at Casterglass for Christmas."

"By myself?" Seph had returned with a touch of asperity, and her sister had wrinkled her nose.

"Well, no. I thought with Oliver."

"You thought Oliver and I would spend Christmas together?" Seph had asked, surprised. If she hadn't made that immediate leap, why had her sister?

"It seemed as if you both were kicking around…" Olivia

trailed off, blushing, and Seph had a sudden, more-than-sneaking suspicion. "Wait, did you all *plan* for Oliver and me to be alone?"

"Er…not quite?"

"What is that supposed to mean?"

Olivia shrugged uncomfortably. "I mean, when all the plans were falling into place for everyone, naturally we thought about you and Oliver… No one wanted you to be left on your own."

"No one actually said anything about that to me," Seph retorted.

Olivia rolled her eyes. "Well, we wouldn't, would we? That would be one sure way to scupper the whole thing."

"Wait…" Seph stared at her sister as realisation crept up on her. "You mean, you guys have been trying to *match-make*?"

"No, no, of course not," Olivia said quickly. "More like…let nature take its course." She smiled brightly. "So, where are you going, then?"

"Prague," Seph replied. "With Oliver."

She didn't know how she felt about her family having contrived to manage events so she and Oliver would spend time together. They'd been subtle enough that she didn't suppose it really mattered, and she'd felt both gratified and annoyed by their meddling in equal measure. In any case, now that she was finally in Prague, her family having all left Casterglass for their various destinations, she didn't want to spend a moment more thinking about the past, or Caster-glass, or any of the Penryns. She was here with Oliver, and she wanted to make the most of it.

"So, what should we do first?" she asked once they'd gone through immigration and picked up their bags. "Check into the hotel?" She was trying to sound knowledgeable even though she'd never travelled anywhere before.

"Yes, and then maybe have a wander, explore the city?" Oliver smiled at her, and Seph tried not to show how nervous she felt, as well as excited. The logistics of travelling had kept them occupied now, but the next three days stretched in front of her, tantalisingly unknown. Would they have enough to talk about? Would sharing a room be weird? Would it feel romantic? What if it didn't?

They took a taxi from the airport to their hotel, in a narrow town house overlooking the ancient and iconic bridge. As Seph stepped into their room, her breath left her in a rush. It was cosy. Very cosy. There might be separate beds, but they were side by side, with only inches in between, and the bathroom was only about three feet away. They would be living cheek by jowl for the next three days, and all sorts of awkward scenarios exploded in her brain—getting changed, going to bed, going to the bathroom. What if she farted on the toilet? He'd most certainly hear her. What had once seemed potentially romantic she feared had suddenly become the opposite.

"It didn't look quite this small in the photos," Oliver

said with a little laugh as he set down his bag. Seph didn't reply and he glanced at her uncertainly. "This isn't too weird, is it?"

"No," Seph said quickly, too quickly.

Oliver grimaced. "It is weird, isn't it? We should have just stayed at Casterglass, rattled around the castle."

"No," Seph said again, meaning it more this time. "I didn't want to stay at the castle. I've spent every Christmas of my life there. I wanted to do something different. Be someone different." She took a deep breath and then a daring step closer to him. "This is perfect, Oliver. Thank you."

His expression softened and she thought, with a thrill, that he might reach for her hand—and *then* what, she didn't know—but there was a sudden, loud knock on the door. Oliver turned to open it while Seph released a pent-up, shaky breath.

"Towels," he said wryly, as he dumped a stack of fresh towels on the bed. "Shall we explore the city before it gets dark?"

"Yes. Sounds good."

Minutes later they were strolling down the Charles Bridge, admiring the stalls of Christmas trinkets, as twilight settled softly on the city. With its many spires and red-tiled roofs, it looked like something out of a fairy tale, cloaked in a soft, dreamy violet. A lamplighter was lighting the gas lamps along the bridge by hand, which Oliver told her was an age-old tradition in the city.

"Or so I read on the internet," he admitted sheepishly, and she laughed.

"Let me guess. You saw a YouTube video."

"Hey," he replied with pretend severity. "Don't knock it."

They walked until it grew dark, and then went back to the hotel to change for dinner, which Oliver had reserved at a nearby restaurant. In the end, it wasn't that awkward to change; Seph took her clothes into the bathroom, and came out in the same sweater dress she'd worn to that first party, borrowed from Olivia. Oliver's eyes gleamed with admiration as she did a self-conscious twirl.

"I love that dress," he told her, and she thrilled to his words, all the while wondering if something was actually happening between them, or if this was just a weird friend thing. Was romance unfurling like a flower between them, or was this trip her being firmly friend-zoned? She had no idea, couldn't even guess, because she had so little experience with men, with romance, with dating.

But she hoped. Oh yes, she hoped.

Dinner was in a cosy little restaurant on a quiet, cobbled side street; they ate roast pheasant in wine and dumplings, washed down with a bottle of red so Seph's head swam, in a pleasantly dizzy way, as they chatted and laughed in the candlelight.

"When will you ask your uncle about Pembury Farm?" she asked, emboldened by the wine. She propped her chin in her hand as she gazed at him across the table. "You must want to know one way or the other, whether you can keep it or not."

"Ye-es," Oliver replied slowly as he rotated his wine glass between his long, lean fingers. "I do, but I also don't. Because if he tells me no, then that's it, and I'm not sure I could stand it."

"What do you think he'll say? Really, deep down?"

Oliver hesitated and then gave her a bleak look that tore at her heart. "I think he'll say no," he admitted heavily. "In fact, I'm quite sure of it. There's no real reason why he would give it to me, when he has a perfectly good son."

"But you said Jack doesn't want it—"

"No, but he wants the money. And I think my uncle is willing to give it to him. He's taken him on holiday now, because he works so hard in the City. Maybe he's telling him right now that he's going to sell."

"I'm sorry." Impulsively—and perhaps because of the wine—Seph reached across the table and clasped Oliver's hand with hers. She'd meant it be a quick, commiserating touch, nothing more, but he twined his fingers with hers in a way that felt shockingly, wonderfully intimate.

"Maybe it would be for the best," he said slowly, his lowered gaze on their clasped hands. "All my life I've tried to be good enough for my uncle. Tried not to let all the little slights hurt, done my best to prove myself to him. Maybe I need to finish with that. Be my own man. Find my own way in the world, away from Pembury."

"But Pembury is part of you." She could hear both the longing and anguish in his voice, and it made her ache.

"Still, perhaps it shouldn't be. You've been wanting to escape Casterglass. Maybe I need to escape Pembury."

"I don't know," Seph replied slowly. "Yes, I've wanted to leave Casterglass, because I've never known anything else. It felt stifling, but it also felt safe. I think Pembury Farm is different for you. You've been away, and you've chosen to return. Maybe I would too, with Casterglass, if I'd been given the choice."

"And maybe I won't be given the choice," Oliver replied, looking up with a crooked smile. "If my uncle decides to sell, I'll have to do something different."

"And what would that be?"

"I honestly don't know. My whole life has been tied up with that house, but in the end that's all it is. A house." He hesitated, and then his fingers tightened a tiny bit on hers. "Althea suggested I keep working at Casterglass for a couple more years."

"Oh?" Seph's voice came out diffident, although she wasn't sure why. Didn't she want Oliver to stay at Casterglass, with her? Wouldn't that be wonderful? And yet something about it gave her pause.

Oliver gave her a level look, clearly sensing her reticence. "How would you feel about that?"

"I...don't know," Seph admitted slowly. "Not about

having you there, but being there myself."

He raised his eyebrows in surprise. "You're really thinking of leaving?"

"If I ever found the courage," she replied, not realising until she'd said the words how much she meant them. "I don't want to live in that poky and mean little cottage all on my own for the rest of my days." Just the thought of it made a shudder go through her.

"Staying at Casterglass doesn't have to mean that," Oliver pointed out reasonably.

"I know, but…" Seph shook her head slowly. "It *would*, even if I didn't live at that cottage. Maybe that doesn't make sense," she confessed in a rush, "but I feel like staying there will always be stifling. It's the nature of the place—for me, anyway—and the life I've had there. If I want to be different, truly different, I have to leave." She sat back in her seat, her hand still clasped with his, as the realisation thudded through her. "I didn't fully know that until I said it," she told him wonderingly. "But I know now that it's true."

"So you'll leave Casterglass." Oliver's voice sounded heavy.

"Maybe. Hopefully? I don't know." She shook her head. Their fingers were still twined, and she wondered what any of this meant for them—Prague, her future plans, their clasped hands. What, exactly, was going on here? She was working up the courage to ask—and taking a while with it—when Oliver stirred, slipping his hand from hers.

"Come on," he said, as he raised one hand for the bill. "Let's walk back to the hotel. The moon is out, and we can walk across the bridge, maybe have a drink in the bar."

✳

As THEY STEPPED outside the restaurant, the air was frosty and clear, a full moon glimmering above the bridge like scenery in a play. It was all so perfect, and yet Oliver's heart ached. He thought of what Seph had said, about needing to leave Casterglass. He understood, of course he did, but it didn't make it hurt any less. Where could he fit into that picture?

He knew he wanted to, and yet he had the horrible sense that he was going to fall prey to that old cliché—*if you love someone, let them go…*

But he didn't want to. He felt as if he'd just found Seph, and with her, found himself. He didn't want to let any of it go, and yet did he really have a choice? Seph was finally finding her wings, starting to spread them. Who was he to clip them, with expectations about a future together, either at Pembury or Casterglass?

Or, he wondered as they headed back across the bridge, was he just giving himself an excuse not to risk his heart, because he knew how much that could hurt? *Don't say anything… Let her be free…and stay safe.*

Was that really how he wanted to be?

Seph paused halfway across the now-empty bridge, resting her hands on the ancient stone balustrade. "Look," she said softly. "Isn't it beautiful?"

Mist was rolling slowly across the river, wispy and ghost-like, like shreds of gossamer, trails of smoke, the water underneath glinting beneath the moonlight. Somewhere along the narrow streets, a church bell tolled the hour.

"It's so magical," Seph said softly. "I feel like I have to pinch myself, to make sure it's real." She turned to him, her expression turning almost fierce. "Thank you for giving this to me. For going ahead and booking it. I never would have done it on my own, and I—I'm glad I'm seeing it with you."

Oliver felt as if his heart was overflowing with the depth of his feeling. Sod letting her go. He couldn't keep this in. He didn't want to, and he hoped and prayed she didn't, either. "Seph..." he began, but then words weren't enough, and he was reaching for her, his hand slipping, drawing her towards him.

Her eyes widened almost comically as she came, her breath coming out in a surprised rush as she stood next to him, their hips and shoulders bumping, their breath mingling in frosty puffs.

"I want to kiss you," Oliver admitted with what he'd meant to be a wry voice but came out full of longing. "Would that be okay?"

"*Oh...*" She sounded so surprised that for a second both his will and his hope faltered. "I thought...I thought we were just friends..."

No. *No, no, no, not again*, Oliver thought with a lurch of

despair, a rush of humiliation. He'd got it all wrong again, laid his heart on the line and for what? He could hardly believe it. Why did he have to be such a *chump*…

And then Seph was smiling shyly, reminding Oliver of a rose unfurling, as she stepped even closer to him. "I didn't dare hope…" she whispered, and his heart felt like a sunburst exploding in his chest as he took her in his arms.

"Me neither," he said, and then he kissed her. Her lips were soft and hesitant under his as Oliver pulled her more tightly to him. The feel of her slender body against his, the way her mouth opened under his…if all he had for the rest of his life was this moment, then it would be enough.

Well, not quite. But almost. It felt like a perfect kiss, in a perfect place, and even though he knew neither of them had any idea what the future could possibly bring—for Pembury, for Casterglass, for each other—he would happily stay here, with Seph in his arms, forever. Forget the future, he thought as he kissed her again. Let them just have this.

After a few delicious seconds they broke the kiss, blinking at each other shyly. The smile Seph gave him was wondering and incredulous, and made Oliver grin goofily back. Yes, they had this, he thought, as silently, by mutual agreement, they walked hand in hand across the bridge, and maybe that was all they'd have. He would just have to let it be enough.

Chapter Seventeen

SEPH BLINKED SLOWLY in the early morning sunlight filtering through the curtains of the hotel room. In the bed next to her Oliver was still asleep, his hair delightfully tousled, his mouth slack. She recalled that kiss all over again and a warmth spread through her body, a joy in her heart. It really had been the most wonderful thing.

Afterwards they'd walked back to the hotel and had a drink in the bar just as they'd planned, but they'd kept grinning at each other, and even letting out a silly little laugh every once in a while, as if neither of them could believe they'd actually kissed.

It wasn't until they'd headed upstairs for bed that Seph had started to panic a bit. Yes, they'd kissed, and maybe they were even dating, but what did Oliver actually expect? When it came to this particular department, she was as inexperienced as it was possible to be, and she knew she wasn't ready to change that situation any more than they already had. Fortunately, Oliver seemed to understand that perfectly, for he ushered her into the room like a gentleman, let her have the bathroom first to change before changing himself, into a very respectable pair of pyjamas that made him look, rather endearingly, like a middle-aged man.

Then he'd climbed into his bed while she'd climbed into hers, smiling wryly. "We've moved from a first kiss to being an old, married couple," he told her teasingly. "*Very* old."

She'd laughed and he'd lain on his side, facing her. "We don't have to rush anything," he'd said seriously. "I know you're still figuring what you want out of life, and you're most likely not ready to decide whether I might be in it. But if we can keep spending time together, and I get to kiss you on occasion, well, that's enough for me."

His words, so sincere and heartfelt, had brought a lump to her throat. He was letting her call the shots, and for that she was very grateful, but at the same time part of her wanted to clamber out of her bed and into his, whatever the consequences. She didn't, though, because sense prevailed, but she did reach for his hand.

"That sounds pretty good to me," she said, and he'd smiled and squeezed her hand. They'd fallen asleep, still holding hands, and she'd woken up this morning feeling happy and grateful and excited for the day, but also wondering what the future might hold for either of them. *Both* of them.

"Good morning." The smile he gave her was both warm and wry, with a hint of self-consciousness. "I didn't consider this whole morning thing. Bedhead and bad breath…not for the faint of heart." He scrambled up to a sitting position to stretch, and Seph had to draw her eyes away from his surprisingly broad chest, the tantalising glimpse of taut stomach as he'd lifted his arms above his head. Wim Hof had nothing on him when it came to six-packs, she thought with a thrill. She'd been too shy to look at him properly when they'd been swimming, but now she was conscious of his body, his nearness. Of wanting to crawl right into his arms.

"What shall we do today?" she asked as she scooted up to sitting, as well.

"I thought we could explore the city a bit more, see the Christmas markets. We have *The Nutcracker* this evening, and then tomorrow is Christmas Eve."

"Christmas Eve." She shook her head slowly. "Casterglass seems so far away right now."

"It is far away," Oliver returned with a smile. "Over a thousand miles." He paused, his smile fading as he gazed at her seriously. "Does that feel like a good thing?"

"Right now, yes." Seph had no idea what the future held—for her, for Oliver, for Casterglass—but she knew she was glad to have some distance, as well as some perspective. "I'm ready for new adventures," she told him, and while Oliver smiled in return, she got a sense of hesitancy from his expression, even of disappointment. Anxious doubts swirled in her stomach. Was he regretting their kiss last night? No, surely not. He'd held her hand while she'd slept. The first thing he'd done was smile at her this morning. She was just feeling insecure because this was all so new.

"You can shower first," Oliver told her gallantly. "And I'll make coffee." He nodded towards the tea and coffee caddy on the bureau.

"Thank you, that's very gentlemanly." She smiled and then scooted out of bed, grabbing her clothes before hurrying into the bathroom.

If she'd been worried that things would be awkward between them now that they'd kissed—and she had been—Seph was wonderfully relieved to discover that actually things weren't awkward at all. They chatted easily over breakfast, and when they went outside to explore the Christmas markets, Oliver caught hold of her hand and they walked along, hands clasped and swinging, as natural as she could possibly please.

They spent the day wandering around the Christmas markets in Old Town and Wenceslas squares, picking up some trinkets and ornaments for those back home, trying Czech specialties such as *vdolky*, a sweet doughnut topped with cream, as well as schnitzel. Later they warmed up in a café with hot chocolates, before they returned to the hotel for dinner and then to change for the evening's performance.

As Seph tidied her hair and decided to go wild with a slick of lip gloss, she felt a pang of sorrow, that it was already ending so quickly. Tomorrow was Christmas, and their last day in Prague. They'd decided to go to the midnight mass at

St Vitus Cathedral in the city centre tonight, and then tomorrow they would tour Prague Castle before having a rather romantic dinner on a river cruise. And then back home to Casterglass and normality... Why did she feel such a wave of dread at the thought?

These few days had opened something up inside her that she hadn't realised had even existed—a sense of hope, of possibility that her life could be so much more than she'd once thought it could. Maybe she could go back to school, get her A levels, even go to university. Why not? She was only twenty-three, after all. She pictured herself living in some city somewhere, a young woman about town, but something about it jarred and she wasn't sure what. She couldn't quite see it somehow, even with this new sense of hope, yet she knew she wanted her life to change, just as she had changed.

Oliver tapped on the bathroom door. "Ready?" he called, and she turned away from her reflection and then opened the door with a smile.

The Nutcracker was as magical as she could have hoped, and Seph was rapt through the whole three hours, enchanted by the dancing, the music, the sheer wonder of it all. The bells were tolling eleven o'clock when they emerged from the theatre and hurried to the cathedral for the midnight mass. The inside of the church was huge, soaring and majestic, flickering with candlelight, and they listened to the service while holding hands—they'd been doing a lot of that lately—as a solemn sense of the season crept over her.

When they walked back in the early hours of the morning, Seph found her steps becoming slower and slower as they reached the hotel. Oliver turned to her with a smile, his eyebrows raised.

"Tired?" he asked, and she couldn't help but sigh.

"Yes, but it's also…I don't want this to end."

His smile faded a bit although his tone remained philosophical. "You don't want to return to Casterglass?"

"It's just been so magical," Seph explained. "I feel like I've been given a whole new world and I don't want to hand it back."

"So do I," Oliver replied quietly, "and I don't want to hand it back, either." Then he tugged her by the hand and kissed her so gently and sweetly that Seph's heart swelled with both happiness and hope. "This doesn't have to end when we go back," he ventured as he broke the kiss, gazing into her face with an endearing earnestness. "Does it?"

She gazed back at him, her lips still tingling. "You mean…us?"

"Yes, us." His expression turned intent, almost fierce. "I know this trip has been like a moment out of time, but that doesn't mean we have to be. That is…if you wanted to? Have this go on after we get back to Casterglass? Be together, I mean."

A teasing smile curved her mouth. He looked both intent and nervous, and it endeared him to her all the more. Just like her, he had his doubts and insecurities. Together they were overcoming them.

"Seph?" he asked, and she realised she'd just been staring at him, her heart so full it was hard to speak. Even so, she couldn't resist the opportunity to tease, just a little.

"Wait," she asked, putting her hand on her hip and cocking her head. "Are you asking if I want to be your *girlfriend*?"

He let out a little laugh, colour touching his cheeks before he squared his shoulders. "Why yes, I guess I am."

"Well, then, the answer is yes," Seph told him with a smile that felt as if it could split her face. "One hundred per cent yes."

The grin that broke over his face in a wave of relief made her laugh too, and then he was kissing her again, his arms tight around her, and Seph thought she could have stayed there forever. This was where she wanted to be, she realised, whether it was at Casterglass or in Prague or anywhere else. In Oliver's arms.

❇

COMING BACK TO Casterglass felt both hard and good, Oliver reflected as he turned down the sweeping drive. They'd had an amazing time away, and he was sorry it was over. Yesterday, on Christmas Day, he and Seph had exchanged presents—she'd bought him a button-down shirt 'in the one colour he didn't have' and he'd given her a carved wooden bracelet he'd found at one of the Christmas markets, because it reminded him of her own amazing workmanship. They'd both been shy about giving their gifts, hanging their heads a little, until Oliver had laughed and asked what were they like, both of them finding this so new and wonderful and yes, a little bit scary.

Seph had laughed, shaking her head. "Well, I've never given a Christmas present to anyone except my family before," she told him. "I've never had a boyfriend before, you know." She blushed a little, and Oliver held her hand. He wasn't overly experienced in the romance department, it was true, but he appreciated just how new and strange this all was for someone like Seph, who had spent a lot of her life hiding in the shadows.

It was new for him too, because already he knew he'd never felt like this before, about anyone. Audrey, his girl-friend from Oxford, paled into insignificance compared to how he felt about Seph.

Last night they'd lain in their separate beds, holding hands and talking until the wee hours of the morning. Seph had told him about how she'd been bullied in sixth form, a quiet, passive-aggressive kind of cruelty that had made her quit after year twelve. Oliver had told her about getting a job rather than going to university, out of a need to prove to his uncle that he could pay his way, and then applying to Oxford as a mature student at the ripe old age of twenty-two.

They'd shared each other's disappointments and griefs in a way that had felt honest rather than self-pitying, and when

Oliver woke up in the morning, groggy after only a few hours of sleep, he realised he was still holding Seph's hand.

But now they were back at Casterglass, with everyone descending on the castle—and them—in the next few days, and Oliver was afraid they wouldn't be able to hold on to what they'd had when they'd been by themselves in Prague. He knew Seph had a complicated relationship with her family at the best of times, and their relationship would only further that complication. He imagined Althea's knowing looks, Olivia's teasing remarks... How would Seph respond to all that? To him?

And then, of course, there was the whole question of the future...not just their future, but Seph's. If she left Casterglass...well, where did that leave him?

"You've been awfully quiet," Seph remarked as Oliver parked the car by the stables.

He let out a sigh as he turned to her with a weary smile. "Just tired, I think."

"It looks like Rose and Sam are back," she said, with a nod to the car he'd parked next to. "I thought they were staying a whole week."

"Travelling must be pretty challenging with babies in tow." He paused and then said, "Are we...telling people?"

She eyed him uncertainly. "Telling people?"

"About us. That, you know, we're dating." Which made him feel about sixteen. What he felt for Seph, what he wanted from their relationship, was so much more than *dating.*

"Do you want to?" she asked, and the uncertainty in her voice made him answer a bit more robustly than he might normally have.

"Yes. Definitely yes."

"Good." She nodded. "I do, too. Even if I'm sure everyone will make a big fuss about it." She pretended to shudder, but she was smiling. So was he.

"All right, then," he said. "Let's do this."

As they came into the castle's kitchen, they were greeted first by the noise. Oliver tried not to react to the screeching as they both gaped at Rose and Sam pacing the room, each with a wailing baby in their arms.

"What's happened?" Seph asked in alarm. Sam was looking exhausted, Rose manic.

"We came back early," she said as she frantically jiggled Bea—or was it Michaela? "They both got colic. At least I think it's colic. They've been screaming all the time."

"And they won't sleep," Sam added, his voice a deadened monotone. "At all."

"Oh dear." Oliver glanced at Seph, who was looking like he was feeling—torn between wanting to help and fleeing the scene. So much for the big announcement they were going to make, to fanfare and fuss. Rose and Sam were too overwhelmed to notice or, most likely, care about their new couple status.

"Is anyone else home yet?" Seph asked.

Rose shook her head. "Mum and Dad are coming home tomorrow, Olivia and Will the following day, and Althea and John sometime after that." She jigged the baby again, to more wails. "I just don't know what to do," she said, her tone wobbling. "She's not hungry. I just fed her. She won't stop crying…"

Seph glanced at Oliver, then put down her bag and held out her arms. "Do you want me to take her?"

Rose's lips trembled and she pressed them together. "But you just got back…" Oliver could tell she was desperate to thrust the baby into Seph's arms.

"You look like you need a sleep," Seph replied. "The two of you. Oliver and I can manage for a couple of hours."

A couple of *hours*? He tried not to let his alarm show on his face. Neither of them was very good with babies, especially very small, screaming ones.

"Are you sure?" Rose asked, while Sam was already jettisoning Michaela—or maybe Bea—into Oliver's arms. He took hold of the baby, floppy head and all, with as much alacrity as he could.

"Yes, we're sure," Seph assured both Rose and Sam.

Within seconds both Rose and Sam had disappeared upstairs, and Oliver and Seph were left holding two very loud and unhappy babies.

"You're a saint," Oliver told her as he attempted to jiggle Michaela—or was it Bea? "I am not."

"It's only for a few hours," Seph reminded him. "We'll

manage."

"Will we? Who do I have, anyway?"

"Bea. She always has a purple bow in her hair, and Michaela has pink."

Seph smiled, draping the baby over her shoulder and rubbing her back with an ease Oliver admired—and envied. "How did you get to be such an expert, all of a sudden?"

She laughed. "Fake it till you make it, I suppose. I've watched the twins a little in the last month, when Rose has needed a sleep."

"I had no idea."

"You've been busy."

"So have you."

She shrugged, and he felt a rush of—what? Dare he call it love? Something warm and wonderful, anyway, a deep affection for this woman whose depths he was still getting to know.

"So how do I make her stop screaming?"

"Deep knee bends help. And they get you fit at the same time."

He laughed, and then tried it, going into a deep squat with the baby in his arms. After ten, she started to quiet. After fifty, his thighs were burning.

"How long do I have to do this?"

"Until she falls asleep, or burps, or both."

"Yikes."

They were both doing the deep knee bends, babies on

their shoulders, as they shared a conspiratorial grin. Oliver felt he would be happy doing anything, as long as it was with Seph.

After about twenty minutes, the babies both finally fell asleep. Neither he nor Seph were brave enough to risk putting them in their Moses baskets, so they crept upstairs and very carefully, very gently, sat together on the sofa, the babies snuggled on their chests.

Before today, Oliver had had something of a phobia of infants, or at least a heathy fear of them. Having got these two to sleep, though, and seeing how Seph cuddled Michaela, he felt something besides fear, something like possibility. He wasn't ready to become a father, no way, but he could see himself becoming one eventually, which was more than he'd ever thought about before.

Cuddling his own child, teaching a son or daughter to walk, to ride a bike, to love Pembury Farm just like he did. He'd never thought about any of those things before, but now he was, especially when he looked at Seph.

She smiled back at him sleepily, her chin resting lightly on Michaela's head. As carefully as he could, so as not to disturb Bea, Oliver reached for her hand and laced his fingers through hers.

"This wasn't how I saw this day going," he admitted ruefully, "but it has its pluses."

"They are sweet, really."

"Especially when they're asleep."

"True."

They smiled at each other, and Oliver gently squeezed her fingers. Yes, he was actually pretty perfectly content right now, in a surprising way. Then, just as he was about to relax into the sofa, the baby a warm, heavy weight on his chest, Bea stirred, lifted her tiny head, and started screaming afresh. Oliver shot Seph a look of pure panic as she rubbed Michaela's back.

"Start up with those knee bends again," she advised him, and with a groan, Oliver struggled up from the sofa.

Okay, so he was not perfectly content, but he realised he was still smiling, even as he did deep squats for the sake of the baby…and all because he was with Seph. She, he was coming to realise, was the most important thing in his life right now. Not Casterglass, not Pembury, not the past or the future or anything like that. Just Seph.

Chapter Eighteen

"**S**O HOW IS the loved-up life?"

Seph rolled her eyes as Althea ventured into her workshop with a canary-eating grin on her face. "It's fine," she replied, managing to sound only a *little* bit terse. She really was changing.

"Seriously, I want to know," her sister persisted. "How did you and Oliver get together, anyway? What made him finally declare himself?"

Seph shrugged, her eyes on the order form she had been completing, for a load of butternut wood for her new sculpture. She was calling it *Grace* and it was going to be lots of sinuous curves and long, straight lines, flowing together, creating a pattern. "I don't know that he declared himself," she answered cautiously. "It's just that we spent a lot of time together, and got to know each other, I suppose." Since returning from Prague three weeks ago, they'd spent just about every moment they could together—sunset walks, afternoons chatting over coffee or playing board games, the occasional stint of babysitting, and one whole, gorgeous day away at Windermere, which had been brilliant and really quite romantic.

"Do you think it's serious?" Althea asked, and Seph hesitated, her gaze still on the order form.

Her family had been surprisingly unfazed by her and Oliver's romance, not that they'd announced it from the rooftops. They'd just quietly gone about their business, and everyone had more or less accepted their new status without anyone having to say anything outright. This was, in fact, the first time Althea or anyone had come fishing for details. She supposed she ought to be grateful that they'd been granted that long a reprieve.

"I suppose it is," she answered, her tone still cautious, although the truth was, she didn't actually know—at least not for sure. *She* felt serious about Oliver, and when she caught him looking at her with that lovely, blazing intent in his green eyes, well, she was pretty sure he felt serious about her, as well. At least she hoped he did. But the truth was, his internship was coming to an end in less than a month and they hadn't talked about the future at all. Would he return to Pembury? Seph had looked on Google Maps and the drive from Casterglass to the North Yorkshire Moors was two and a half hours. Not impossible, but not all that great. Would they keep up some sort of long-distance relationship? And what about her own life, the plans she'd barely begun to formulate?

Since returning from Prague, she'd been flirting with

ideas of moving on from Casterglass, maybe going to university, opening a new chapter of her life, but she hadn't really got any further than that. She hadn't made any decisions, and she wasn't even sure how to begin.

"I asked Oliver if he wanted to stay on at Casterglass for another year," Althea said. "He said he'd think about it."

Seph nodded. "I know."

"That would be good, wouldn't it? Considering?"

"Maybe." She and Oliver hadn't talked about him staying on here, either, and Seph still wasn't sure how she felt about it. Did she want to spend the rest of her life at Casterglass, even with Oliver here, too? The answer, she thought, was probably no.

"Why only maybe?" Althea asked. "The two of you at Casterglass sounds perfect, to me. He can manage the orchard and you can do your woodworking. If things continue to get serious between the two of you, you could move into the cottage I showed you." Althea gave a little shrug as if to say 'sorted.' And it did sound sorted—but in a way Seph knew she didn't want. As much as she was coming to care for Oliver—and she was—she did not want to spend the rest of her days here. She knew that right down in her bones.

Seph took a deep breath and met her sister's narrowed gaze squarely. "Althea," she began, and her sister raised her eyebrows.

"Uh-oh, that sounds serious, and not in a good way.

What is it?"

"I don't want to move into that cottage." Seph kept her voice firm even though inside she was quaking. She wasn't good at confrontation; her former sulky stuff had run away from it, time and time again, but she knew she needed to talk to her sister about this.

"Okay," Althea replied after a moment, sounding slightly hurt but like she was trying to hide it. "That's fine. It was just an idea, after all. There are loads of other places you could live on the property, I'm sure—"

"No." Seph shook her head to forestall her sister from mentioning all the hidey-holes she could be put up. "I don't want to live in some converted barn or potting shed or dovecote or whatever else you're thinking of."

"Well, not a *potting* shed," Althea protested, and now she sounded affronted. "Do you want to stay in the castle itself? Because we might be able to manage that, if we change the plans for Sam and Olivia's flats—"

"No," Seph cut across her. "I don't want to stay at Casterglass at all."

Althea's mouth opened and closed soundlessly. "What?" she finally asked faintly. "What…what do you mean?"

Everyone else had found their home at Casterglass, Seph knew, but she had, conversely, found her freedom. "Before you came back," she told Althea, "Dad was thinking of selling this place."

"Yes, I know—"

"And I was thinking of moving. I didn't even know where, just somewhere new. Somewhere I've never been, which is basically anywhere."

"But..." Althea was looking completely flummoxed. In any other situation, it would have been comical, but Seph felt too emotional about this even to smile. "You love Casterglass," she protested. "Out of all of us, you love it the most. You've been here the most—"

"Because I never had the opportunity to leave. Or if I did, I wasn't brave enough to take it. Well, I am now. I hope I am." She squared her shoulders while Althea stared at her, dazed.

"Where would you go?"

"I don't know. I've thought about getting a degree, or a job, or even travelling. I've saved up some money, since I never do anything or go anywhere."

Althea blinked slowly, clearly trying to absorb everything Seph had said. Seph still needed to absorb it herself. Even though she'd said as much to Oliver, saying it out loud to Althea felt different. More serious. "And where does Oliver fit into this?" her sister asked finally.

"I don't know," Seph admitted. "His heart is back at Pembury, but I think it's likely his uncle will sell the farm and give the money to his cousin, so that's probably a non-starter, unfortunately."

"So he'll be free."

"Yes, that's true." And yes, she *had* considered whether

Oliver would be willing to strike out with her, wherever they decided to go. Paris, Prague, or maybe only as far as Preston. Somewhere new…together. But she was way, way too scared to mention that kind of commitment after just three weeks of dating, even if she felt so sure. She didn't know if Oliver did.

"Both of you leaving Casterglass." Althea shook her head slowly. "What about the woodworking shop? And the orchard?"

"I'm sure you can get other people to manage them."

"But you love woodworking, Seph." Althea's gaze narrowed. "Don't you? Or is that something else I've got the wrong end of the stick about?"

Seph managed a small laugh. "No, I do love woodworking, and who knows, maybe one day I'll come back to Casterglass and take it up again. Or do it somewhere else, if the mood takes me." She shrugged, savouring all the possibilities, even as they scared her a little. "You, Olivia, and Sam all got the chance to go somewhere else, be someone else—at boarding school, at university, as an adult. I never did."

Althea frowned. "I thought that was your choice."

"Sometimes it was, and sometimes it wasn't." Seph doodled a bit on her form, her gaze lowered. "I felt trapped here, trapped by my own inexperience and lack of confidence," she confessed quietly. "But that's changing."

"Because of Oliver?" Althea guessed shrewdly, and Seph looked up with a smile.

"He certainly has had something to do with it."

Althea let out a sigh and then straightened her shoulders. "Well, I'm glad, for your sake. For both your sakes. I had no idea… I always assumed you as cosy as a pea in a pod here." There was an uncharacteristic note of uncertainty in her sister's voice, a lilting apology. They'd all assumed that, Seph knew. Perhaps it had been easier for them. And, she acknowledged, perhaps it had been easier for her.

"Sometimes I was," she told Althea. She'd learned enough about herself to realise living at Casterglass hadn't been all bad, as she might once have thought it was. She'd relished the freedom here, and she'd learned how to be strong. It was just that now she was ready to try something new.

"Okay, well…" Althea shook her head slowly. "I'm happy for you, I guess. I mean, I must admit, I'd rather you stayed here, but that's just me being selfish. You need to do what's best for you, and if leaving is that, if you're sure, then…I want that for you."

"Thank you," Seph said quietly. She knew it cost her sister something to admit as much.

"When…when will you go?"

Seph's heart lurched a little at the thought of actually leaving Casterglass. It had all felt like a pie-in-the-sky possibility, until she'd actually told someone about it. "I don't know. There's no rush. I'm still thinking, and I suppose I need to see what happens with Oliver."

"He's crazy about you, you know."

Seph blushed, unable to keep a sloppy smile from spreading over her face. "We'll see."

"He is, Seph. You've got a good one there."

Seph could only nod. Yes, she knew she had a good one in Oliver, of that she was absolutely certain. But if neither of them seemed ready or willing to talk about the future, how long would it last?

❄

OLIVER GAZED DOWN at the text from his uncle, reading it for the sixth time. *How about this weekend for a visit? We need to talk.*

His stomach roiled unpleasantly. So, this was it. His uncle must be about to sell Pembury Farm. Oliver had known it was coming, deep down, and yet he'd still hoped. Dreamed, although tangled up in those hazy visions of him as master of Pembury was being with Seph. How would those two go together? Well, now he wouldn't have to wonder or worry. They wouldn't.

With a sigh he slid his phone back into his pocket and stared unseeingly out the window of the little office where Althea had him updating the castle's website. Over the last two months he'd become part of Casterglass, and yet it still wasn't home. It wasn't Pembury.

But maybe Pembury wasn't home any longer, either.

In any case, he decided as he squared his shoulders, this would make it easier to move on. If Pembury was no longer an option, then he'd have to do something else. He had no idea what, but he'd think of something. He knew Althea's job offer was still open, but he sensed that Seph didn't want him beholden to Casterglass in the same way she had been. She wanted to move on, but the question was, did she want to be with him? And if so, where?

The last few weeks had been wonderful, but their relationship still felt too new to start having those kinds of deep, forever kinds of discussions, even if Oliver felt like he was ready. He knew what he wanted: Seph, at Casterglass or wherever else took her fancy. But not, he feared, at Pembury.

It was just as well, he reminded himself. Seph didn't want to be tied to a place, whether it was Casterglass *or* Pembury. At least now they would both be free. And yet he ached to show her the place he loved above all else, the only home he'd ever known.

An idea took hold, rooted down. Could he… *Would she?*

There was only one way to find out.

Taking a deep breath, Oliver rose from his seat and went to find Seph.

She wasn't in her workshop as she usually was, and the rooms of the castle's addition where most people hung out—kitchen, sitting room, bedrooms—were empty, at least of Seph.

"Looking for Persephone?" Violet said as she brewed a revolting-smelling cup of herbal tea in the kitchen. "I believe she went out to the walled garden. She seemed quite…thoughtful." Violet cocked her head, her gaze sweeping over Oliver, and with a murmured thanks he hurried out the door, wanting to avoid one of Violet's oddly perceptive pronouncements.

Although it was nearing the end of January, the day was fresh, the sky clear, with the tiniest hint of spring in the air. The walled garden's bushes were bare and neatly tended, but gorgeous clusters of snowdrops, like tiny white bells, were scattered across the emerald-green grass.

After wandering the twisting brick paths for a few minutes, Oliver finally found Seph sitting on a wrought-iron bench near an old summerhouse, her face tilted to the sun. She opened her eyes as he came closer, smiling at him in easy affection.

"I was just enjoying the peace and quiet."

"Sorry, am I disturbing it?" he asked with a wry smile.

"You know you're not." She scooted over on the bench, to make room for him. "Were you looking for me?"

"Yes." He tried not to gulp in his nervousness, and Seph gave him a curious look.

"That sounds awfully serious."

"Not serious, *per se*." She patted the bench and he sat down next to her. "I just wanted to ask you something."

"Oh?" Her tone managed to be both guarded and hopeful, and he wondered what she was thinking he'd ask. "My uncle would like me to come back to Pembury Farm for a visit next weekend. He said we needed to talk."

"You think he's going to tell you he's selling it?"

"I'm pretty sure he is." Oliver suppressed the inevitable sigh this thought caused him. "But what I wanted to ask you was, would you go with me? To Pembury, for the weekend? I know it'll be gone soon but I'd love for you to see it." To fall in love with it, the way he had, even if it couldn't be his. *Theirs.* "And meet my uncle, too," he added, an abashed afterthought, because perhaps he should have thought of her meeting him before seeing the house, but it was definitely the house that felt the most important. The house it seemed he couldn't have.

It took Oliver a few seconds to realise Seph hadn't replied. She was looking at him with a mixture of apology and dismay, and his stomach cramped because her expression definitely did not bode anything good.

"I mean, obviously only if you want to," he said, forcing the words out. A few months ago, he might have tripped over himself to make excuses and apologies, but now he found he couldn't stomach it. He couldn't hide his hurt. "But if you don't, then..." The usual words, *that's fine*, simply wouldn't come. "Then you don't," he finished flatly.

"Oh, Oliver..."

She sounded so sorry, that he couldn't stand it. He rose from the bench, so his back was to her as he raked a hand through his hair. "I knew it was a big ask," he managed. Even if he'd been ready for it. "If you don't feel we're at that stage..." He didn't know how to finish that thought in a way he could bear.

"It's not that," she said quickly. "Oliver, please! Look at me. You're jumping to all sorts of conclusions, thinking I don't want to go with you—"

He made himself turn around and look at her. "Do you?"

"Yes!" She bit her lip. "And no. Of course, I want to see a place that's important to you. You've told me so much about Pembury Farm. But…I'm not good in social situations. I'm not…" she shrugged helplessly "…normal."

He couldn't help but feel a bit exasperated at what sounded like an excuse. "Seph, you are definitely within the realm of normal, whatever that even means."

"But I'm not! I can't do chitchat. Social niceties escape me. I'm trying, but with strangers… I don't know." She looked up at him, her blue-green eyes pleading with him to understand. "I'm scared," she said quietly.

Oliver stared at her, her wide eyes, her nibbled lip, and realised she was serious. For a few minutes there, in his own hurt and insecurity, he'd forgotten hers. "Okay," he said at last. "I get that. And if you're not up for it, that's…that's okay."

She stared at him for a few seconds while he waited for the relief to break across her face, but it never did.

"Okay," she said at last. "I'll do it." She made it sound as if she'd agreed to have her tooth pulled out with a pair of rusty pliers, and he found himself smiling.

"You will?"

"Yes. Because it's important to you. And because I want to, even if I'm terrified."

"You don't have to—"

"Look, if we keep giving each other excuses, we'll be here all day. I'll do it. Let's go. Next weekend, you say?"

"Yes."

She nodded resolutely, now like someone facing the guillotine. "Okay. We're on."

Oliver sat next to her on the bench and gathered her up in his arms. He loved the way she nestled against him, her head tucked under his chin. "Thank you, Seph. This may be the only time you see Pembury Farm."

"I want to see it. I want to share in anything that's important to you. It's just...not always easy."

"I know." His arms tightened around her. He was glad she was going, even if he dreaded the thought of what his uncle was almost certainly going to say. At least then they'd both be free, he told himself, to face whatever the future held...together.

Chapter Nineteen

T HE NORTH YORKSHIRE Moors looked a lot like Cumbria, but gentler. Seph stared out at the rolling green hills and valleys streaming by and tried not to hyperventilate. According to the satnav, they were less than ten minutes from Pembury Farm. And she was terrified.

She'd agreed to accompany Oliver because she knew how important it was to him, but that didn't mean she liked the idea, or was looking forward to the weekend in any way, shape, or form. Chitchat with strangers…being scrutinised…having to answer all sorts of questions about her unconventional childhood… It sounded like a living nightmare.

Yesterday Olivia had given her a crash course in basic etiquette, something she'd never actually learned the way her siblings had. How to hold her teacup, the right fork to use, when to put your napkin on your lap. Seph's head had been buzzing with it all when Althea had come into the musty dining room that the family never used and rolled her eyes.

"Oh, for heaven's sake! She's not going to meet the

queen."

"Oliver's uncle is the grandson of an earl, though, isn't he?" Olivia pointed out.

"An extinct title, and in any case, Seph is the daughter of a baronet. Look, Seph." Althea had faced her straight on, brisk but smiling. "Just be yourself. I know that sounds stupid and clichéd, but I actually mean it. If you can't be yourself, there's no point, because your relationship with Oliver won't last. Trust me, I should know. I acted like some airhead socialite for Jasper's sake, and I was more or less miserable for twenty years." For a second Althea's expression tightened; Seph knew the years lost to her philandering ex-husband still stung, even though she was over-the-moon happy with John. "If you can't be yourself, then you don't want to be with him," she stated with quiet definitiveness.

"I can be myself with Oliver," Seph protested. "It's his uncle I'm worried about."

"Well, who cares about him, anyway," Althea replied with a careless wave of her hand. "Especially if he's selling the family farm."

Well, *she* cared, Seph thought as they drew ever closer to the farm in question. As much as she'd appreciated Althea's encouragement, she was still going to be spending the whole weekend with Oliver's uncle, and even though Oliver's feelings were complicated when it came to that particular relationship, Seph knew the man still mattered to him. The weekend stretched ahead of her, a minefield of awkward moments and mishaps, ones that could even threaten to destabilise her relationship with Oliver. Everything between them was so new, after all; what if a weekend away was the worst thing ever, not just for her, but for *them*?

"Seph, it's going to be okay," Oliver said, reaching over to pat her hand. "Don't panic."

"How do you know I'm panicking?"

"Because you're clinging to the door handle like we're about to crash, and I happen to be going thirty miles an hour." Seph managed a sheepish smile as Oliver slowed down and put on his indicator. "And here we are. Welcome to Pembury Farm."

His voice held a warm note of pride and Seph took a deep breath as she turned to look at the lane Oliver was turning down. It was a narrow track that wound its way through the mellow hills, towards a house of golden stone nestled in a copse of beeches, with a small pond out front and an orchard out back, a few barns and outbuildings alongside.

"I know it's not a patch on Casterglass Castle," Oliver told her with a wry grimace, but Seph just shook her head.

Yes, the house was a lot smaller, with a row of only six mullioned windows rather than a round dozen, glinting in the afternoon sunlight, and not a crumbling turret in sight, but there was something so homey and welcoming about it all that already she felt more at ease, if, admittedly, only a bit.

"I can see why you love it," she said, and he gave her a quick, searching look.

"Can you?"

Seph glanced back at the house, looking so snug and contented in its little spot. Everything looked neatly tended without being intimidating or showy; there was a comfortableness to the whole place that she instinctively liked. "Yes, I think so."

"I'm glad." He reached over to touch her hand briefly before they pulled up in front of the house; the front door, facing the pond and the road, looked the more imposing but was clearly little used; just like at Casterglass, everyone went through the back door, straight into the kitchen.

A couple of springer spaniels raced out as Oliver climbed out of the car and he bent to fondle their ears. "This is Clover, and this is Patch," he said, introducing them both while they gave Seph a very thorough sniff. "They're absolutely ancient, but they still have loads of energy."

Seph gave them each a tentative pat; her family had never had dogs growing up, as her parents had been far too absentminded to take care of pets along with children, but as the two spaniels frolicked and pranced around her, she thought she might like to have a dog, one day. A dog like these ones.

"Oliver."

Seph saw Oliver spring to attention, a look of wary alertness coming over his features, and she turned to face the man who had come out of the kitchen to greet them. He was, she thought, more or less exactly what she'd expected him to be, without even having realised that she'd formed a mental image—bluff, red-faced, dressed in an old jumper, baggy cords, and expensive-looking brogues. He had an air of shabby gentility crossed with City banker, and he clapped Oliver rather heartily on the shoulder before turning to Seph.

"And you are—Persephone?"

"Please, call me Seph. Everyone does." After a second's awkward pause, Seph held her hand out to shake, knowing it would be clammy with sweat. Simon Belhaven shook it with the same heartiness with which he'd clapped Oliver on the shoulder.

"Lovely to meet you. Let me show you your room while Oliver puts on the kettle."

He led them both into a kitchen that reminded Seph of Casterglass even though it really was rather different. Yes, there was the same sort of big Aga-style cooker, and a long, scrubbed table, a clutter of boots and a deep-silled window over the sink overlooking the garden, but it was a fifth of the size, and not nearly as messy. There was a hominess to it that the kitchen at Casterglass lacked, perhaps because of its size or maybe just its mess.

The dogs trotted in after them and threw themselves in front of the Rayburn with an exhausted, dramatic flair that made Seph smile. Simon was beckoning her up to the back stairs that led directly from the kitchen, a set of narrow, twisting stairs that had Seph stooping so she didn't bump her head.

"I've put you in the back bedroom, with views of the orchard. Oliver mentioned he's been doing up the orchard at Casterglass? I had a look at the website, and I was most impressed by all I saw and read."

"Oh, yes," Seph replied after a second's startled pause. She realised that after everything Oliver had said, she hadn't expected Simon Belhaven to be quite so friendly. "I'm sure Oliver will be pleased to know," she added, and Simon shot her a quick smile.

"Oliver's never been much of one for accepting praise," he remarked drily, which also made Seph wonder. She had a feeling that Simon Belhaven's view of his relationship with Oliver might differ from Oliver's. But then, hadn't she found that with her family? Her perspective was, in the end, just that—her perspective. Althea, Olivia, Sam, her parents...they all had their views, their own experiences, just as Oliver had his. It wasn't necessarily the entire truth of a situation, just one person's perception of it...a realisation that had helped her make peace with her own unconventional childhood. Perhaps Oliver needed to make peace with his.

"I'll leave you to freshen up," Simon told her, after showing her into a pretty, cosy room with white-painted furniture and a bedcover in intricate broderie anglaise. "Then we can all sit down with a cuppa."

"Sounds wonderful," she replied, and Simon gave her a quick smile before he hurried downstairs.

After he'd left, Seph let out a gusty sigh. This wasn't going to be as bad as she'd thought, she realised. Simon was friendlier than she'd expected, and already she had a sense that she was going to like Pembury Farm, its cosy shabbiness without Casterglass's eccentricity. From the window, the view of the orchard was lovely, even in February, the trees neatly tended and pruned, the hills beyond rolling away to the horizon.

Yes, this could all be quite pleasant. It was a shame, though, if this turned out to be her only visit.

❅

"It's good to see you, Oliver."

Oliver turned from the kettle as Uncle Simon stood at the bottom of the stairs, having just shown Seph up them. Nerves fluttered in his stomach, and he fumbled for a couple of mugs. "It's good to see you, as well."

"It's been too long."

Oliver shrugged; he'd spent the whole summer at Pembury, mucking out the barns and trimming the grass, trying to show his uncle how he could take care of the place. Loving every inch of it. As he turned back to glance out the window, he felt that familiar ache of longing. He knew these hills and valleys, these fields and forests, like the back of his own hand, his own heart. He'd wandered them as a lonely schoolboy, had built castles-in-air dreams about the farm when he was in charge, had poured sweat and even blood into the day-to-day managing of the property—mowing the grass, dredging the pond, repairing the outbuildings. In the farmhouse itself he'd whitewashed beams and painted rooms, replaced rotten floorboards and even, with the help of trusty YouTube, fixed the dodgy electrics.

To say Pembury Farm was part of him was an understatement; it was the very fabric of his soul. It had been his family when he'd felt abandoned or ignored by everyone else. Yet he knew he could never explain that to his uncle.

"I'm sorry I didn't ask you to come with us, up to Scotland for Christmas," Simon said, ducking his head in apology.

"It's all right. I didn't expect it," Oliver replied. He turned his gaze back to the kettle as he poured boiling water into the big blue teapot he remembered from his childhood.

"I know, you wouldn't," Simon said on a sigh. Oliver had no response to that. There had been a few family holidays he hadn't been invited to over the years; there had always been a good reason, of course. Jack and Simon needed alone time; Oliver was busy at university, or with work. Last-minute tickets, and there were only two. He'd got used to it, he supposed.

"I was hoping we could talk," Simon began, but just then Seph came downstairs, looking uncertain, and Oliver leapt at the chance to forestall what he knew was going to be The Big Discussion.

"Ah, Seph. Tea? Then I thought I could give you the

grand tour."

"Sounds fab," she said cautiously, and Oliver glanced at his uncle.

"We'll talk later," he replied with an easy shrug, and they all sat down to tea and chitchat, with no mention of the future of Pembury Farm at all.

AFTERWARDS, SIMON WENT into his study while Oliver headed outside with Seph. The sky was starting to darken to violet at the edges, the sun hitting the top of the hills, but there was still enough time to show her the main sights. Wearing wellies and with the dogs trotting at their heels, they headed for the orchard first.

"Your uncle seems nice," Seph remarked. "And fond of you."

"Yes, in his own way." Oliver shrugged. "I never thought he wasn't, not really, just that I wasn't…" He paused, not wanting to sound self-pitying. "All that important, I suppose."

"Perhaps you're more important than you think," Seph replied quietly.

Oliver glanced at her. "What makes you say that?"

"It's something I've realised with my family." She paused, her forehead furrowed as she tried to organise her thoughts. "I made some assumptions, I think, in believing that people didn't care. And it's true, they could have showed they cared more. My father said as much to me recently, and he apologised to me for being…well, forgetful, I suppose. But I didn't help matters, because I never said it bothered me. I pushed people away, as you very well know." She gave him a wry grimacing sort of smile. "But maybe you've pushed people away too, in an entirely different way? By being too…too *nice*. Too understanding. Acting like nothing ever bothered or hurt you."

"That's true. I did act like that," Oliver said slowly as he considered the matter. He'd known he and Seph were alike, even though they showed that likeness in very different ways, but he hadn't thought about how their families could be alike, too. How you could push people away by being too easy-going just as much as by being too snarky, and how that could make people decide not to try.

"You might be right," he conceded after a moment. "Although I'm not sure how much it matters in the end. My uncle will sell Pembury and move to London regardless."

"You can't be sure—"

He gave her a bleakly pragmatic look. "I'm pretty sure." Determined to shake off his dour mood, he slipped his hand into hers. "But let me show you all of Pembury, and why I love it."

They spent the next hour strolling along bridleways and exploring the little wood, walking along the pond and skirting the barns, as twilight drew in like a violet curtain being pulled across the sky. Even though he knew it was futile, Oliver couldn't help but paint a picture of what he wanted to do—the big barn that would be a wedding venue, the cider press in the shed, the tree house playground he could build in the wood.

"It wouldn't be anything as big as Casterglass—"

Seph squeezed his hand. "You don't need to compare it to Casterglass."

"I know." He grinned wryly, shaking his head. "Sorry."

"Don't be sorry. This place is magical." She paused to survey the view—fields rolling gently to a twilit horizon. "I can see how it would be the kind of place that burrows into your soul. A place to put down roots, to…" She paused, and then finished, "To be happy."

Oliver had the sense she'd been going to say something else, and he wondered what it was. To settle down? To have a family? His mind buzzed with promising possibilities, before he remembered that none of it mattered, because shortly his uncle was going to tell him he was selling up.

"Come on," Oliver said, tugging gently on Seph's hand. "We should head back to the house before it gets dark."

✳

THE TALK—OLIVER THOUGHT of it in capital letters—came that evening, after they'd had a cosy supper around the kitchen table—a cottage pie from Waitrose, but Simon had never been a good or even adequate cook—and Seph had thoughtfully retired early, leaving his uncle to get out the port and two crystal tumblers, while Oliver followed him into the front room.

A few minutes later they were both settled in the old, embroidered chairs flanking the fireplace, with a generous inch of port to sip as the fire crackled merrily and the dogs stretched out on the old, worn rug in front of it, groaning in weary pleasure.

It was all very comfortable and civilised, Oliver thought with an ache of longing, a spurt of bitterness, for news he knew was going to break his heart.

"This conversation has been overdue," Simon began. "I know you've been concerned about the future of Pembury Farm, as I have been, for some time."

Oliver raised his glass to his lips before putting it down again, his stomach writhing too much to drink. "Yes, I have," he replied quietly.

Simon gazed around the sitting room, with its smoke-stained beams, its sagging window frames, the old chintz sofa, and the Turkish carpet that had faded to a muddle of pastels. "I do love this place," he said softly. "I always have. I never even wanted the grand estate, lost before my lifetime, of course. Just this place."

"Yes." Oliver found his throat was becoming thick. His uncle really did sound like he was about to break bad news—no surprise, of course, and yet now that the moment had come, it hurt, almost unbearably. If they both loved this place so much, why couldn't they keep it? The only thing standing in their way was about a million pounds and Jack's admittedly understandable need for his inheritance.

"And I am getting older," Simon continued, rehashing familiar territory, since this was all stuff they'd discussed last summer, when Oliver had made his big pitch to take the farm on himself, and his uncle had remained less than convinced. A lot less. *I know you mean what you say, Oliver, but it's such a big job...* "I can't manage the stairs as well as I once used to," he continued, "and it's been difficult to keep on top of all the maintenance, especially without you here."

Oliver thought of the parade of holidays and summers he'd spent at Pembury over his school and university years, working himself to happy exhaustion. "Yes," he murmured, because there wasn't really anything else he felt he could say.

"As you know, my hope was always that Jack would be willing to take this place on. I know he's been keen to make his mark in the City, but one of the reasons I took him to Scotland was for one last attempt to get him to love this place like I do. Like you do." Simon sighed and shook his head. "I think, as hard as it's been, I've finally accepted that he doesn't, and he never will."

"No," Oliver murmured in agreement, his voice little more than a whisper, his throat too tight to say anything more. *Here it came...*

"And so, I've reached a decision," Simon announced, his tone heavy with import. He took a sip of port and then put down his tumbler to give Oliver a serious, intent look that he found he couldn't look away from, even though he wanted to. He knew he really didn't want to hear what was coming next. "And I admit, it wasn't an easy decision to make," his uncle continued. "In many ways, it goes against the grain, but it also, I'm glad and thankful to say, feels wonderfully right. And I hope, Oliver, even though I know that it affects you the most, you'll agree with me."

Oliver shook his head helplessly, knowing he would never agree with the decision to sell Pembury. *I'll be free*, he reminded himself numbly. *Seph and I will both be free, never having to tie ourselves to a place...*

The thought, in that moment, was not remotely cheering.

"And so I've decided to give Pembury Farm to you," Simon finished, and Oliver stared at him for a good ten seconds before he finally replied, his mind buzzing.

"Sorry—what?"

"I'm signing the farm over to you, Oliver. Jack has agreed. He was surprised at first, I admit, but he saw the sense in keeping Pembury in the family. He'll get a good lump sum of money, anyway, which I am afraid is what he was most concerned about."

"But..." Oliver shook his head slowly. He couldn't quite believe it. No, sod that, he couldn't believe it at *all*. "I thought you'd decided to sell."

"I'd certainly considered it," Simon replied seriously. "And I'm afraid, in order to give Jack an inheritance, I can give you the house, and only the house. No money to keep it running, so it might very well end up being a millstone around your neck. I'm also putting in the proviso that if you sell it in the next three years, Jack will receive ninety per cent of the money. After that, the percentage goes down each year until, after fifteen years, he would receive nothing. I know that might not seem fair to you, but Jack was concerned you might take the house and flip it. I told him nothing could be further from your mind, but..." Simon trailed off, spreading his hands. "It was a way to keep the peace, or at least an approximation of it. It hasn't been easy for any of us."

"I..." Oliver shook his head again. His mind was still spinning. "I don't even know what to say. I thought you'd asked me to here to tell me you were selling the place. I was sure of it."

"I thought you might think that." Simon paused, the expression on his florid face turning both reflective and sad. "I don't think you've ever realised or trusted just how much I care about you, Oliver. I know things haven't always been easy—Jack was a bit of a bully, I'm fully aware of that. And having Penny leave when you were only twelve—well, she left me, but I know you must have felt like she left you, as well."

Again, Oliver found he couldn't speak. He had no idea his uncle had been so perceptive. He'd assumed, meanly perhaps, that he hadn't seen any of those nuances, hadn't read any of those emotions.

"I…" He had no idea what to say; he felt too overwhelmed for words.

"I should have been more attentive, more…affectionate." He grimaced. "The truth was, I wasn't entirely sure what to do with you, before Penny left, and then after…everything felt too hard. That's my fault," he emphasised. "Make no mistake about that. I should have done better. Been better."

"It's—" Oliver wasn't sure how to finish that sentiment, and in any case, his uncle didn't let him.

"The point is," he pronounced, "I want you to have the place. I've seen how you've loved Pembury Farm since you were a small boy. This place is in your bones, your blood. I've always seen that." He roused himself, sitting forward in his chair as he met Oliver's dazed gaze with a wry smile. "So, do you feel you really can take this place on, Oliver? You're up for the challenge? And Persephone is, as well, if things are as serious between you as I suspect they are?"

The smile he gave him was genial, but Oliver was suddenly stricken. *Seph.* How on earth would she feel, knowing he'd been saddled with a big house and zero income, and one he couldn't even sell if he wanted to, not without incurring devastating loss? Talk about being tied to a place. It would be a ball and chain, one he'd welcome gladly, gratefully, but Seph had always made her feelings clear. She wanted to see the world. She wanted to spread her wings. She didn't want to be tied to yet another meandering old pile.

How could he ask her to sign up for something she

hadn't asked for, didn't want? And yet if he were forced to choose between Seph and Pembury…well, it would be like choosing between his heart and his soul. A person needed both to survive…yet Oliver feared he would have to lose one or the other. The question was, which one would it be?

Chapter Twenty

"OLIVER, WHAT IS it?"

Seph paused in their meander through the fields surrounding Pembury. It was Saturday afternoon, and Oliver had seemed either preoccupied or in a daze since this morning. Or really, she thought, since his uncle had talked to him last night; at least she'd assumed they'd talked. Over supper Simon had made vague noises about wanting to have 'a proper chat' and so Seph had pleaded tiredness and excused herself after the meal. She'd expected Oliver to fill her in before too long, but he hadn't.

This morning he had looked thoughtful and withdrawn, which made her heart ache. Simon must have told him the farm was going to be sold. When she'd found a quiet moment to ask about it, though, he'd shaken his head repressively.

"I'll tell you all about it later."

She assumed he simply didn't want to talk about it, and she didn't particularly need a post-mortem of the painful discussion, and so she'd left it, happy enough to explore

Pembury some more, sit by the roaring fire, play a cutthroat game of Scrabble, and generally enjoy herself, somewhat to her own surprise.

Now, however, they'd been walking for over an hour, exploring the nearby lanes and fields, the dogs alternately frisking at their heels or racing ahead, and Oliver had been in a morose sort of silence the whole time. Seph wasn't fed up, not *exactly*, but she did want to know what was going on.

"Is it the house?" she asked. "Do you want to tell me about it?" *Finally*, she added silently, as she waited for Oliver to speak.

He gazed out at the distant fields, glinting with wintry sunlight, his expression both remote and troubled.

"Something has happened," he said slowly. "Something I never expected."

"Which is?" she asked with a touch of exasperation, when it seemed as if he wasn't going to say anything more.

Oliver turned to look at her squarely. "Uncle Simon is giving me Pembury."

"What!" For a second Seph could only stare at him in confusion. Why on earth was he acting so grim, then? A bubble of laughter rose up in her throat and she swallowed it down. "But, Oliver, that's—"

"I know how you don't want to be tied to a place," he continued hurriedly. "And here I'll be, tied a hundred and ten per cent, because he's giving me the house but no money to run it, and I won't be able to sell it even if I wanted to.

Not for a while, anyway. Not," he clarified, "that I want to sell it. But it will be a big responsibility. A liability, even. I have no idea if I'll be able to make it solvent."

"Yes, but—"

"And I don't want you to feel beholden," he continued, his tone growing in determination, a hard, settled look coming over his face. Seph's excitement for him began to morph rather quickly into a deep dismay. "To Pembury, or to me. This relationship we've had, it's quite new. I know that. It would be wrong of me to ask you to sign up to something like Pembury, when we're still just really getting to know each other."

"Wrong of you," she repeated woodenly. Was he actually breaking up with her? He'd been handed Pembury and he realised he didn't need Casterglass—or her—anymore? Was that what was going on here?

"Yes," Oliver replied, and now he sounded firm, decided. "I've been going over it in my mind, and I…I don't want to ask that of you. It wouldn't be fair."

Amazing how he could couch dump her in such noble language. Seph felt herself retreating, like some kind of animal into its protective shell, safe from pain. Her shoulders squared and her lip curled upwards, almost of its own accord.

"If that's what you've decided," she replied with a shrug, as if it didn't really matter one way or the other, as if her heart wasn't splitting right in half—although not splitting, nothing as clean and easy as that, one swift break. It was withering and shrivelling inside her, turning into some dead, desiccated thing. Without waiting for him to reply, Seph turned on her heel and started to walk back towards the farmhouse.

"Seph, wait!" Oliver jogged after her. "I'm trying to look at this fairly—"

"Yes, so you've said." Her voice was hard, and she strove to moderate it, to make it sound like she didn't care, the way she always had, before she'd made herself change. Well, sod changing, she thought savagely. It sucked. Putting yourself out there, caring about people... It was just as she'd always feared. She got hurt. Much better to walk away first, the way she was doing now, except Oliver had been the one to start, and it was too late. She *was* hurt, even if she was trying not to show it.

It wouldn't be fair of me.

Whatever.

"Seph," Oliver called. "I'm sorry..."

She didn't bother to reply, just kept walking.

❇

SHE SPENT THE next few hours in her room, crying into her pillow and hiding from Oliver. Not exactly the way she'd thought this weekend would turn out, but then it had been full of surprises. Oliver was getting Pembury after all, and it had made him realise he didn't need her. Two things she'd never expected. She thought of all his flowery words, when he'd invited her on this weekend in the first place—how he wanted her to see it, how important she was to him. How he'd showed her every inch, spun a fairy tale of dreams of what he'd do with the place, and she'd imagined herself there with him, had even, cringingly, almost said it was the perfect place to start a family. Thank goodness she'd kept herself from that, because it had clearly all been bollocks, and it was enough to stem her tears and make her feel angry, which was a lot better than feeling heartbroken. Well, not a *lot* better, but at least a little, except of course she was still heartbroken. Heart withered.

Still, after a few hours she felt strong enough, or at least almost, to venture downstairs, her eyes dry and her expression almost personable. She wasn't sure what she was going to say to Oliver but she felt she needed to face him. He, however, looked abject.

"Seph," he began in a low voice as she came to the kitchen table where Simon had laid out all sorts of lovely things from Booths—quiches and cocktail sausages, cold meats and artisan cheeses, along with a crusty baguette. He'd already apologised for not being much of a cook, but in any case, Seph had absolutely no appetite.

She shook at Oliver to forestall him from explaining yet again how *fair* he was being, and they spent the meal in stilted conversation with Simon, who seemed determine to pick Oliver's brain about how he would set the farm up as a commercial enterprise. Seph listened in silence as he talked about the orchard, and cider making, a campsite and turning the big stone barn into a wedding venue, just as he's told her earlier.

They were all ideas he'd learned at Casterglass, and she was glad he would be able to implement them here, or she would have been, if he hadn't chosen to cut her out of his life as ruthlessly as if he'd been wielding a pair of scissors. Now that he had Pembury, he didn't need her. It really did seem as simple as that.

Simon retired early after what felt like an interminable supper, and while Seph just wanted to run away back upstairs, she knew Oliver wouldn't let her. They would have to have some sort of final conversation, which she was dreading.

"Seph, please," he said, as she got up to clear the plates from the table. "I don't think we've talked properly about this."

She shrugged, her back to him as she started to stack the dishwasher. "It sounded as if you'd said all you wanted to say." She turned back to face him, leaning against the counter, her arms folded.

He regarded her unhappily. "It sounds as if you've made up your mind."

"*I've* made up my mind?" Seph repeated in disbelief. "You're the one who decided for me." She whirled around to stomp upstairs—exiting stage left was her specialty, after all—but Oliver grabbed her arm.

"Wait," he said, gently turning her around to face him. "*Wait.* What is really going on here?"

"You've decided now that you have your precious farmhouse, you don't need me," Seph fired back, too hurt and angry to keep it all in any longer. "Without giving me so much as a say-so! Well, *fine*. Pembury isn't a patch on Casterglass, anyway." It was a stupid insult, spoken out of her hurt, but she regretted it instantly.

Oliver shook his head, a look of impatience flitting across his face. "But you don't even want to stay at Casterglass. You told me you didn't want to be tied to a place. You want to try new things, move somewhere, maybe even go to university."

All pie-in-the-sky dreams that felt as far away as ever, not impossible but not as wanted. "So?" Seph demanded.

"So, I wasn't trying to decide for you, Seph. I was trying to…set you free."

❄

OLIVER FELT AS if he were going crazy. It was as if he'd been privy to only half a conversation, and Seph had filled in the other half without him. Or, he realised, maybe it was the other way round. In any case, he feared—and hoped, too, strangely enough—that they'd both seriously got the wrong end of the stick. This was all a misunderstanding, wilfully born out of their own hurt and confusion, and Seph *hadn't* been breaking up with him this afternoon.

"Set me *free?*" she sneered, her lip curling, her eyes flashing hurt as she yanked her arm from his grasp and folded her arms. "Wow, thanks. Thanks so much."

Oliver stared at her, looking as prickly as she ever had. They'd both, he was starting to realise, stayed true to lamentable form. As soon as the stakes had risen, the first hurdle they'd come to, they'd fallen back into their old, safe, and unhelpful ways.

He'd tripped over himself, far too eager to please and handing her an excuse to walk away on a plate—hadn't he done that too many times in his life already?—and Seph had retreated to her usual self-defence, a surly sullenness, a faked indifference. All because they'd both been afraid to take a risk with their hearts.

Or, he wondered, was he completely misreading the situation and he was about to get his poor, trembling heart ruthlessly stomped on? Well, better to love and lose than never love at all, he decided recklessly. These things were clichéd for a reason, he supposed; they held some truth, at least, even if it wasn't the most palatable at the moment.

"Seph," he said to her, his voice as firm as he could make it even though his offered heart was beating wildly, "I want nothing more than for you to throw your lot in with me and Pembury Farm. Working this place together, like I was talking about yesterday—that would be my dream. But what I was trying to say, in a very clumsy way, this afternoon, is that I recognise it might not be your dream. And it wouldn't be fair of me to ask you to make it so, just because we're together. I didn't want you to feel beholden, and I suppose I was giving you a get-out clause, in case you needed one." His own form of self-protection.

She stared at him for a few seconds, her gaze wide, her mouth opening soundlessly. "I thought you were breaking up with me," she said finally.

Oliver shook his head. "I thought *you* were breaking up with *me*."

"I think I was, sort of," Seph admitted in a low voice. "Before you delivered the death blow."

"I didn't want to ask you to commit to something you didn't want or weren't ready for," he explained. Although he wasn't as noble as that; the truth was, he hadn't wanted to be rejected. Hurt. "So I couched it in terms that left me with some self-respect, I suppose," he confessed, wanting to be completely honest, "because I didn't want to beg, because of my pride as well as not wanting you to feel guilty." He shook his head, annoyed by the way he'd reverted to form. At least he realised it now. They both did. "I guess I failed on both counts."

"Do you really want me to work Pembury with you?" Seph asked slowly, and Oliver realised just how much he'd given away with that heartfelt statement. He'd been talking about a lifetime and he had no idea what she felt about *that*. Once again, he felt exposed, and the urge to backpedal was strong. Still, he managed to keep himself from it, this time.

"Well, yes, I do," he told her. "In time. Like I said, our relationship is pretty new, but it's also pretty great. And the truth is…" He took a deep breath. He'd never said these words to a woman before, and it felt like jumping off a cliff, going into freefall, hopefully being caught. "I'm in love with you."

Seph's cheeks went pink, and her lips parted again, with no sound coming out. "You…are?" she finally whispered.

Oliver nodded, on firmer ground now. Very firm. "Yes." It was actually a relief to say it out loud, as well as a joy to feel it, to let himself feel it. He'd offered his heart on a plate and he didn't quite know if she'd accepted it yet, but at least it was out there. He loved her. It was simple, it was wonderful, it was true.

"I…love you too," Seph whispered.

The relief made his shoulders sag and the joy, his heart swell. "Then maybe we can face the future together, whatever it holds. I didn't get a chance to say it this afternoon, but my next line was going to be if you really felt strongly about it, I could give up Pembury." He'd come to that conclusion pretty soon after his uncle had offered it to him; it had felt, strangely, both heart-breaking and heart-healing. Pembury mattered to him, but Seph mattered more, and that felt both good and right.

Seph's face softened, suffusing with love in a way that filled him with wonder. He thought he'd never tire of her looking like that, at him. "Oliver," she exclaimed softly, "I know how much this place means to you. I would never ask you to do that—"

"And I would never ask you to live a life you didn't want to," he replied. "Neither would be right or fair, for either of us."

"I've never said I wouldn't want to be at Pembury," Seph told him. "It's true that I've spent a lot of my life feeling bitter about being stuck at Casterglass, feeling like my parents loved the castle more than they loved me, but that was a child's perspective. I've learned a lot more now, and I realise there were a lot of good things about growing up at Casterglass."

That was heartening, but he wasn't sure how much it changed things. "I'm glad, but—" he began, only to stop when she shook her head.

"And," she continued, "when I've pictured my future, I haven't really been able to see it, in some city, going to university or working some job. For better or worse, I think I'm used to being tied to a place. I like feeling a part of things—I think that's what I was resisting again, back at Casterglass. I was stuck there but I didn't feel like I was a part of things. It would be different here, with you."

"It would be," he agreed, still feeling cautious. Could it really be that easy?

"And yes," Seph admitted, "I do want to see the world, certainly more of it than one corner of Cumbria. But more than any of that, I want to be with you. That's...that's where my home is." She ducked her head, as if embarrassed by her sentiment, and once again filled with both relief and joy, Oliver gathered her up in his arms.

"Oh, Seph," he said, burying his face in her hair. "You're my home, as well. I really would give up Pembury for you, you know. I'm not saying it wouldn't be hard, because it would be more even than I can imagine right now, but it would feel right. I'm sure of that. I'd rather be with you than here, any day of the week."

She returned his hug, wrapping her arms around his waist, burrowing into him. Yes, Oliver thought, this was home. The only home he'd ever need. They'd both been searching their whole lives for a place to belong, and they'd finally found it here, with each other.

"And we will travel," he told her, his arms tightening around her. "We'll see the world, we'll explore and have adventures... The last thing I want to do is limit you."

"Oliver, you haven't limited me, you've *expanded* me," she said, her voice muffled against his shoulder. "You've made me believe in myself, which has been...amazing." Her voice thickened a bit and she hugged him once before she leaned back in his arms to look up in his face. "So it's agreed?" she asked. "We're staying together, whether we're at Casterglass or Pembury or somewhere else?"

"Yes." Oliver's tone was fervent. "We're staying together...wherever we are."

They stood there, their arms wrapped around each other,

savouring the moment. Then Seph tilted her face upwards once more, her eyes glinting with mischief.

"So," she asked, "what *will* the future hold, do you think?"

Oliver grinned and kissed her. "Well," he said, fitting her more snugly against him, "I suppose we'll just have to find out. Together."

Epilogue

Two years later

From Country Life:

Two Great Attractions for Summer Fun!

If you're wondering what to do with the kids this summer, then look no farther than Cumbria or the North Yorkshire Moors, and two stunning attractions that offer so much for the whole family. First there's the recently refurbished Casterglass Castle, run by the ancient and venerable Penryn family. Walter Penryn is the twelfth baronet of Casterglass, and his children Althea, Olivia, and Sam all contribute to the running of the property, along with their spouses and many children—Olivia recently gave birth to a little girl which makes number three for her family, Sam two, and Althea just had number four. In addition to the castle itself—ghost tours offered by the fascinating Lady Violet—there is also a walled garden with a treasure trail for children, an ad-

venture playground, glamping site, pottery shop, and orchard. To quench your thirst or pick up a souvenir from the day, there is a lovely café and gift shop on site. Stop by for a warm welcome from all the Penryns!

Over in the North Yorkshire Moors, Pembury Farm is a smaller but no less delightful treasure. With a pick-your-own orchard, playground, petting zoo, and wood-working shop run by Persephone Belhaven (the youngest of the Penryn siblings, and gaining a name for herself as an artist in her own right), it has a delightful home-grown quality. Oliver Belhaven can often be seen around the site, and he offers tractor rides as well as a taste of Pembury Cider, which is known throughout the county. The old barn is the perfect rustic venue for weddings, and catering can be provided. The Belhavens took over running the property a few years ago, and, to add to the fun, are expecting twins in the autumn.

There's plenty to see at both Casterglass Castle and Pembury Farm. Don't miss these two family-run five-star attractions, full of local charm and lots of love!

The End

If you enjoyed reading about the Penryn family, why not try one of Kate's other fun, romantic series: Willoughby Close or The Holley Sisters of Thornthwaite!

Join Tule Publishing's newsletter for more great reads and weekly deals!

Acknowledgements

It takes a lot of people to bring a book to life, and as ever, I must thank all the wonderful people at Tule who help make my books the best they can be. Thanks to Meghan, Cyndi, and Nikki, who manage the practical side of things, and Sinclair, my editor, who is always so encouraging. Also thanks to Helena and Maureen, who diligently spot all the little errors and inconsistencies! And thanks to Jane, who had such a great vision in starting Tule in the first place. I'd also like to thank the good people of St Bees, where I used to live in the Lake District—little did you know how inspired I'd be by such a beautiful place! Thank you for your encouragement and for putting up with my many books set around your village.

If you enjoyed *The Last Casterglass*,
you'll love the other books in the…

Keeping Up with the Penryns series

Book 1: *A Casterglass Christmas*

Book 2: *A Casterglass Garden*

Book 3: *The Casterglass Heir*

Book 4: *The Last Casterglass*

Available now at your favorite online retailer!

More books by Kate Hewitt

The Return to Willoughby Close series

Book 1: *Cupcakes for Christmas*

Book 2: *Welcome Me to Willoughby Close*

Book 3: *Christmas at Willoughby Close*

Book 4: *Remember Me at Willoughby Close*

The Willoughby Close series

Book 1: *A Cotswold Christmas*

Book 2: *Meet Me at Willoughby Close*

Book 3: *Find Me at Willoughby Close*

Book 4: *Kiss Me at Willoughby Close*

Book 5: *Marry Me at Willoughby Close*

The Holley Sisters of Thornthwaite series

Book 1: *A Vicarage Christmas*

Book 2: *A Vicarage Reunion*

Book 3: *A Vicarage Wedding*

Book 4: *A Vicarage Homecoming*

Available now at your favorite online retailer!

About the Author

After spending three years as a diehard New Yorker, **Kate Hewitt** now lives in the Lake District in England with her husband, their five children, and a Golden Retriever. She enjoys such novel things as long country walks and chatting with people in the street, and her children love the freedom of village life—although she often has to ring four or five people to figure out where they've gone off to.

She writes women's fiction as well as contemporary romance under the name Kate Hewitt, and whatever the genre she enjoys delivering a compelling and intensely emotional story.

Thank you for reading

The Last Casterglass

If you enjoyed this book, you can find more from all our great authors at TulePublishing.com, or from your favorite online retailer.

TULE
PUBLISHING

Made in the USA
Las Vegas, NV
02 September 2022

54581554R00164